Not My
WAR

Valerie Anne Hudson

Book cover design and Interior formatting by 100 Covers.

ISBN (paperback) *9798850490089*

Published by KDP

Website: *valerieannehudson.com*

CONTENTS

We must take sides.
Neutrality helps the oppressor, never the victim.
Silence encourages the tormentor, never the tormented.
—Elie Wiesel, Holocaust Survivor

CHAPTER 1

Munich, 1937

The smile on my face froze as an ear-splitting *crack* resounded from across the street.

A gunshot?

Instinctively, I put my hands over my ears, feeling the familiar panic rise up in my throat. Desperately trying to calm my jagged breaths, I told myself to breathe as I pushed away the memory.

You're fine, you're fine. No need to panic.

It had been seven years, but I just couldn't shake off the nightmares. Sudden loud bangs always had a tendency to set me off.

Bringing myself back to the present, I looked across the street to see a group of young men in brown shirts hurling bricks and stones at a shop window.

"What's going on?" I asked my handsome companion.

"It's okay," he said. "Nothing to worry about."

But then, as we watched, an old man—presumably the shopkeeper—was dragged out of the shop. As the men started punching and kicking him, I turned away and put my hands over my face in horror.

Make them stop! I wanted to say. *Why don't you make them stop?*

I didn't say that out loud, though. I was too concerned about looking grown up and sophisticated. But still, I wanted to know why it was happening, in broad daylight, with no-one stopping to help the shopkeeper, who was now moaning in distress as he lay curled up on the ground.

"Why are they doing that?"

"Why? Well, he's a Jew, of course," said Hans with a shrug of his broad shoulders.

I swallowed hard, took a deep breath, and kept walking. It was none of my concern, and I wasn't about to let this little incident spoil my day—a day that was rapidly turning out to be the best in my entire life. Here I was, seventeen years old, walking along the magnificent streets of Munich next to the most attractive man I'd ever laid eyes on. Even in this city, teeming as it was with tall blond Nazi soldiers, in my eyes, Hans stood out like a god.

We had only met a few minutes ago. It was my summer vacation, and I had been invited to spend a month in Munich with my schoolmate Emma while her parents vacationed there. Today, the two of us had come into the city by tram to see an art exhibition. Emma, who had a passion for art, had begged me to come, not that it was necessary to beg. Just to be away from school and teachers, to be in this beautiful, vibrant city without supervision, made me feel giddy with excitement and expectation.

Munich was ablaze with red swastika flags hanging from every public building, a startling contrast to the paleness of the blue sky. The sun was warm on my face, the streets were thronging with soldiers and civilians, and I had never felt so alive.

"I *so* wish I lived here!" I said to Emma as we approached the exhibition.

"Me, too!" she answered. "But I'm starting to think that anywhere in the world would be preferable to living in that miserable English boarding school of ours."

She had a point.

"The Degenerate Art Show" was being held in a building in the Hofgarten park. There was a long queue to get in; from what Emma had told me, the exhibition had been opened by Herr Hitler himself and was supposed to show us the evils of modern art—degenerate because it was an insult to all things German, apparently posing a dire threat to German culture and society. But we were supposed to make up our own minds, Emma said. I knew little about art—little about much of anything, to tell the truth—but didn't at all mind spending an hour or so at the exhibition, especially when there were so many handsome Aryans to admire.

The display of artwork, oddly and crookedly placed on the walls of the dark and narrow rooms, was distinctly unsettling.

"Why doesn't someone straighten them out?" I asked Emma in a whisper.

She put her finger to her lips as if to tell me to be quiet, shook her head, and went back to writing notes on her little pad.

And why aren't any of them in proper frames? I wanted to ask. But didn't.

Stranger still, labels that looked like they'd been written by children were pinned to the walls. My goodness, if I handed in anything that sloppy to my teachers, I'd be in big trouble.

"Nature as seen by sick minds," read one. "Grotesque art," said another. Most of the artists were Jewish.

Soon enough, I realized the slogans were telling me what I was *supposed* to think. One particular painting caught my eye, showing elegant ladies with fur collars in vibrantly clashing purples and pinks. "Ernst Ludwig Kirchner: Street, Berlin, 1913" read the label. "Purchased with the taxes of working German people by the National Gallery in 1920, for twelve thousand German marks."

Smiling to myself, I understood that I wasn't supposed to like this painting because of how much it had cost German taxpayers. Wondering how other people were reacting, I turned around to make instant eye contact with the most handsome man I'd ever seen. His gray-green uniform emphasized the blueness of his eyes, which crinkled around the corners as he smiled at me. I took in his even features, strong jawline, and golden blond hair and lost all interest in the artwork around me. Probably in his early twenties, I thought. Not too old for me at all.

Turning back as nonchalantly as I could to the paintings, I nudged Emma with my elbow, wanting her to see him for herself.

"What?" she asked with a frown. "Just let me write this down."

But when I turned around again, my dreamboat Aryan had disappeared. Trailing along behind my friend, I surreptitiously pulled my compact out of my handbag and touched up my red lipstick. Another coating of mascara was needed, but that was too hard to do with so many people around. But I did manage to comb my hair, wishing I'd worn my pink dress rather than this blue flowered print. With puff sleeves, a large collar, and a white leather belt around the waist, the blue was pretty enough, I supposed. Fashionable, too, but not exactly sensational. Not that I was ever likely to see Mr. Dreamboat again amongst all these hoards of art lovers. Art haters, rather.

By the time Emma had seen her fill, I was so anxious to get out into the fresh air that I stepped through the exit door at a gallop, straight into a solid gray-green wall with brass buttons.

"Excuse me, please. I am so sorry," said my Mr. Dreamboat, stepping back politely.

I looked into those deep blue eyes for the second time that day and was lost for words. Quite unusual for me.

"Don't mind, my friend," said Emma. "She's always clumsy!"

He laughed, then clicked his heels and bowed. "Hans Hartmann. At your service. And this is my friend Peter."

"I'm Louise," I said, recovering myself. I was going to add that everyone called me Lulu but held my tongue. I wanted to appear refined, elegant, worldly; Lulu was a little girl's name. "And this is Emma. Not so much my friend anymore, after that insult!"

"What did you think of the exhibition?" Hans asked. "Incredible, isn't it! Listen, we were just going for coffee. Would you care to join us?"

Would we! One glance at Emma confirmed that we would indeed, and from there, it just seemed natural for me to be walking by his side as he started talking about the evils of expressionism and impressionism. When he paused to ask me my opinion, I was flummoxed.

"Forgive me, but German isn't my first language," I said. "You lost me there." That wasn't quite true because I was fluent in German and understood every word he said. I just didn't want to admit how ignorant I was about art.

"You're not German?" he asked in surprise. "I just presumed because you speak the language so well. Where are you from?"

"That's a difficult question to answer," I said. "I was born in Switzerland. My father was English, my mother is German, and I've spent most of my life at boarding schools in England.

But my mother lives in Paris, so I suppose that's home for me. For now, anyway."

With Emma and Peter close behind, we walked through along the paths of the neatly manicured Englischer Garten and admired the Chinese Tower, which Hans said had been built in the 1700s. And as we passed people picnicking and sunbathing on the grassy banks of the stream, I couldn't resist the allure of that beautiful blue water.

"Emma!" I turned around and pulled her by the hand.

"We have to put our feet in! Come on, let's go for a paddle!"

"No, I don't want to get my stockings wet!" she said.

"We'll take them off, then. Come on!" I laughed and pulled her toward the water. "Hans, Peter, will you come?"

Hans stiffened as a frown creased his forehead. "We're in uniform, Louise. It would be against the rules." But then his frown relaxed into a smile, and as he and Peter sat on the grass, Emma and I ran to the water's edge, peeled off our knee-high stockings, and stepped into the clear, cold water, where we held onto each other, shrieking with joy. It was short-lived. After a couple of minutes, our feet started to turn numb, and we sat on the bank to dry off our feet.

"Time for coffee now, I think," said Hans once we were back in our shoes. He led the way out of the park, and that's when the disturbing incident with the shopkeeper occurred.

"I am sorry you had to witness that," he said, holding out his arm. I took his elbow, basking in the glory of it all. I felt I must have been the envy of every girl in Munich to be walking arm-in-arm with this man. Suddenly realizing he was talking, I tried to pay attention to his words.

"As our Fuhrer says, the mightiest threat to the Aryan race is the Jew. God created Aryans as perfect men, both physically and spiritually. If we die off, the world will become a dark and desolate place indeed."

Desolate indeed, I thought, smiling up at him. He seemed so tall, even though I myself was wearing two-inch heels.

"Jews are ungodly and inhuman," Mr. Dreamboat continued. "They are the embodiment of evil and create disorder. As such, they have to be eliminated."

I wondered briefly if I knew anyone who was Jewish. I thought of the girls in my class at school and wasn't sure. I didn't know what Jews looked like. Perhaps some of our teachers are Jewish, I thought, then decided that the headmistress was almost certainly Jewish because she was evil. Well, evil toward me, at any rate.

Hans continued talking on the same topic, while I only gave him half an ear until he stopped outside a café. The four of us sat at a table outside in the shadow of a huge swastika flag that fluttered gaily over the sidewalk while Hans ordered coffees.

As I tried to sip daintily on the strong, bitter brew, Emma asked if they were off to fight in a war somewhere.

"We're being mobilized first thing tomorrow morning," Hans replied. "We don't know where we're going yet—that's top secret!"

"How exciting!" I said. "I wish I could go!"

"It will be my first time away from home, so I have to admit I'm a little anxious," said Peter. "But we've been training for years with Hitler Youth, so we're well prepared to fight for the Fatherland."

Fight who? I wondered.

"No need to be anxious, Peter," said Hans, making me jump as he thumped his fist on the table. "This is the start of the thousand-year Reich. Our duty to the Fuhrer is clear!"

"Heil Hitler!" said Peter in response, raising his arm in the Nazi salute. I noticed that this seemed to be the way people in Munich greeted each other, even when passing on the street.

Emma said that we needed to get home before her parents started to worry, and we stood up to say our goodbyes to our new friends.

"I'm sorry I have to leave tomorrow," said Hans. "But who knows? Maybe I will find myself in Paris one day. Maybe we'll meet again!"

A comment which I didn't take at all seriously at the time but which came back to haunt me in later years. It seemed that we were destined to meet, one way or another, he and I.

"They're very intense, aren't they?" said Emma of the soldiers as we hurried arm-in-arm toward the tram stop.

"Yes. Fierce, in fact," I replied. "Not to mention incredibly handsome! But I wouldn't want to make an enemy out of those boys, that's for sure."

CHAPTER 2

England, 1937 – 1938

Handsome Nazis were the last thing on my mind by the time I got back to school that September. My last year of school, and I don't know who was more thankful for that—my teachers or myself. Not only was I a poor student, lacking in any academic ability, but I was also a behavioral problem.

As a result, I'd been expelled from two different boarding schools over the course of my life. I suspected that the only reason I was allowed to come back to St. Bernard's Boarding School for Girls was that my mother had paid the headmistress off to take me. Either that or she was blackmailing her. There could be no other explanation.

Boarding schools were the perfect solution for children like me. My father, a British diplomat, was posted at the British Embassy in Switzerland when I was first shipped over to school in England at the age of seven. I lasted at this particular school for four whole years, even though my report cards disappointed everyone except myself.

"Louise needs to learn self-control. Her constant talking and speaking out in class is distracting to the other students."

"Louise needs to think before she acts. Her unruly behavior and unwillingness to follow the rules hinder her ability to learn."

"Louise needs to listen more carefully. She is far too easily distracted from the task at hand."

When I was twelve, my father was stationed at the British Embassy in Paris. And after he died—when the incident happened—I'll admit that my behavior worsened, so much so that I was transferred to Thornhill Boarding School for Girls.

My mother had high hopes that Thornhill would teach me how to become a lady. I was taught etiquette, embroidery, how to be a hostess, the proper way to set a table, and countless other useless topics, which I believed I would never need. Every day was the same routine; every day, I was admonished for fidgeting or speaking out; every day, I was told to sit still, be quiet, and listen.

"You will sit in detention on your own until you come to your senses, Miss Bellingham. You need to reflect on your own behavior."

But that was precisely what I didn't need. In solitude, with no distractions, I would start to feel an almost physical pain. Pain for the loss of my father, pain for what I'd done to my brother, and the pain of knowing that my mother couldn't stand the sight of me. I needed people around me; I craved fun, adventure, excitement.

When I was thirteen, mid-way through the year, the headmistress wrote my mother that I would no longer be welcome at Thornhill. Mother took the unusual step of traveling over to London from Paris to "sort me out," as she put it.

"Louise, you're an absolute disgrace," she said upon her arrival at Thornhill to pick me up. She was speaking in English.

It was a sort of unwritten rule. We would speak English when in England and French when we were in Paris. In England, I called her "Mother," and in Paris, I called her "Maman."

"I cannot believe I've had to come all this way to find you another school. Yet again. Do you not understand how important a good education is? And would it never occur to you that I'm paying hefty fees for these places? You need to..."

I stopped listening when my mother started on one of her rants. I knew exactly what she was going to say, so what was the point? She had another school already lined up for me.

"I'm sending you to a religious school. If they'll have you, that is. Hopefully, they can put the fear of God into you!"

Good in theory. Not so much in practice. We traveled by taxi to St. Bernard's, which was an hour's drive away from Thornhill, just outside of London. When I heard the name of the school—St. Bernard's—I immediately pictured the Saint Bernard rescue dog so well known in the Swiss Alps. Large, fluffy, and lovable. *Maybe this is a sign*, I thought. *Maybe St. Bernard's will save me!* But as we approached the bleak, five-story building, my hopes started to fade. Sitting atop a hill unsheltered from the elements, it looked decidedly damp, dreary, and desolate.

"But I don't like it here," I said to Mother as we entered the building.

"Well, you should have thought of that before, shouldn't you," she replied, rummaging in her handbag for a cigarette.

Dressed in a pale blue two-piece Chanel jersey knit suit, my mother looked exquisite, as usual. With hair that cascaded in dark, shiny waves to her shoulders and long, slender legs, she moved with the elegance of a dancer, even in pale blue high heels. Having grown up in Berlin, Mother spoke English with a slight accent but was also fluent in French, German, and Italian, working as a Professor of Modern Languages at the University of Sorbonne. She looked so out of place in these dull surroundings, I thought. Like an exotic bird.

We were shown into the headmistress' drafty, dingy office and sat in worn leather chairs to wait. My mother sniffed disdainfully.

"There's no question of her turning you down," she said.

"What do you mean?" I asked.

"Just look at the state of the place! They'd take anyone. They really need the money."

Such a comforting thought, but she was right. The headmistress didn't put up any objection to taking me once she clapped eyes on my mother's checkbook.

"I will write you a cheque for the entire year right now. And if any additional fees are required, please don't hesitate to let me know. Louise may be a little, shall we say, 'high-spirited,' but I'm sure…" Here she shot a threatening look at me. "I'm sure she'll soon settle in."

And so it was arranged. Having told the taxi driver to wait, my mother left as soon as she could, graciously turning down the invitation to a tour with the excuse of having to catch her train. A perfunctory kiss on the cheek, and she was gone, leaving behind nothing more than a lingering whiff of Chanel no. 5.

Leaving me to have the "fear of God" put into me.

There turned out to be no *fear* on my part, however, only excruciating boredom. Every day was the same, beginning with morning prayers, followed by a whole hour of religious instruction that made me want to scream. Prunes and porridge for breakfast; soggy cabbage, lumpy mashed potatoes, and grisly meat for dinner; bread, jam, and uninspired cake for tea. Twice a day, we were sent outside for "playtime," where we would huddle as close to the building as we could get, shivering miserably in the wind and rain. As I often commented to the other girls, it was like being in prison.

It didn't take long for me to liven things up. In those early years, my pranks were harmless enough. Hiding all the chalk before math class was especially entertaining since the teacher of that particular subject couldn't cope without it. A good fifteen minutes could go by as she hummed and hawed, searching in cupboards and her desk drawers for a single stick of chalk before sending one of us on a mission to ask for more. On one occasion, I cruelly left her with one tiny fragment, which she valiantly put to use even though it must have been almost agonizing to write with.

On another occasion, I tormented my Religious Education teacher by placing my alarm clock on my desk. Set to go off ten minutes into the lesson, the loud ring sounded sufficiently close to that of the fire alarm for us to all exit the classroom. Only to return several minutes later with the teacher wondering where on earth the ringing noise had come from.

I organized midnight picnics in the dorm, with cake that we'd pocketed at teatime, and on more than a few occasions, we'd sit on our beds in the dark telling each other ghost stories. One night, four of us went on a ghost-hunting expedition into the school basement carrying flashlights. Terrifying but immensely exciting.

Did I get caught? Sometimes, but I was mostly punished for talking in class or not doing my work. The punishment depended on the teacher. I could be made to stand in the corner like a dunce, I could be given a few sharp whacks of the ruler on my knuckles, or in the worst case, sent to the headmistress to be spanked with her cane. I always refused to cry, but those beatings certainly left me sore and reluctant to sit down for a day or so afterward.

I had no shortage of friends at St. Bernard's. The other girls knew how brainless I was when it came to schoolwork, but they never minded sitting next to me, listening to my silly stories, or participating in my adventures. As a result, I was often invited to spend holidays at their homes. Their parents never seemed to object; it was probably advantageous to them to have a friend in tow to keep their daughters occupied.

It was also advantageous to my mother, who was more than happy to agree to these arrangements. Most of the other girls received letters from their parents on a weekly basis. Not me. Two or three weeks would go by between letters from Mother. Written in her spidery handwriting, they were sometimes in English, sometimes in German, sometimes in French, but always short and to the point. First, she would lecture me about my behavior and the importance of an education, then she would give me a brief update about my brother, Jacques, telling me what his latest specialist was advising and what treatments were being recommended.

"The last specialist we saw kept insisting that electro-shock therapy would help, so Jacques underwent that for the first and last time last week. I won't subject you to the harrowing details, but let me tell you, I will not allow him to undergo such barbaric treatment again. Needless to say, I am looking for another doctor."

Reading her accounts of his treatments tore me up inside, bringing tears that no degree of caning could ever have wrung out of me. I think both she and I knew that he would never get better. But my mother would never have acknowledged that. She would have given her own life to help him.

During my last year at St. Bernard's, after my trip to Munich, I smuggled in cigarettes and two bottles of champagne.

"It's important for us to learn how to smoke and drink, you know," I told Emma. "How can we look sophisticated otherwise?" She agreed, so we decided to practice smoking behind the big old garden shed. It made both of us feel sick and green around the edges, but I, at least, was determined to master the elegance of it all. The booze we would share after lights-out. Standing behind the shed for our first smoke, I couldn't help but notice the bicycles lined up there, presumably belonging to some of the teachers. How could I resist? We took two of the bicycles—easy, since none of them were locked, and hid them in a hedge close to the road for later, with the intention of riding them into town that evening.

"What will we do when we get there?" asked Emma. "And how far away is the town, anyway?"

"I have no idea! Whatever looks like the most fun!" I replied.

We never did get to find out how far away the town was, or indeed if there was any fun to be had there for a couple of seventeen-year-old girls. As we giggled and wobbled our way downhill, a car suddenly approached from the opposite direction. Emma swerved into the ditch, I hit the car head-on, and a fuming headmistress emerged from behind the wheel of the car. Barring a few scrapes and cuts, we were otherwise uninjured but shamefaced for being caught.

"Louise," the headmistress said to me later as I stood before her in her office. "You're almost eighteen. Too old for a spanking. But I will be informing your mother. The two stolen bicycles will need to be repaired, if not replaced, and there are scratches on my car which will need to be paid for. In the meantime, consider yourself in detention for the remainder of the year. No more playtimes for you!"

She never found out about the smoking and drinking, though.

I would have happily accepted a spanking over my mother being notified about the bicycle incident. She would be furious.

CHAPTER 3

Paris, 1938

School behind me, I arrived "home" in Paris in July of 1938. After my father's death, my mother moved from our old apartment to a house in the Latin Quarter, close to the University. Since I had spent little time there over the years, it didn't feel like home to me. I had to agree it was a beautiful house, built over a hundred years ago with three stories, high ceilings, and large windows. My mother tells people she chose it for the kitchen and dining room—perfect for entertaining and dinner parties, but of course, the real reason is Jacques. Our old apartment is where our father was murdered, so it was important to move Jacques away from the scene in the hopes he could recover from the shock. At the time, everyone thought that with the move, he would eventually get back to his normal self, but that never happened.

It had been a long journey from St. Bernard's to Paris. A taxi to the train station, the train to Dover, a taxi to the ferry, a turbulent ferry ride across the English Channel, then another train to the Gare du Nord. Fighting my way through crowds of German and Czechoslovakian families at the station, I found a taxi and, out of curiosity, asked the driver what was going on.

"Refugees," he replied with a shrug. "Mostly Jewish, I suppose. They're coming to France to get away from the Nazis."

Ah, that explained it. At St. Bernard's, I'd been kept in a protective bubble, unaware of the goings-on in the outside world. But I knew all about the Nazis and the Jews from my visit to Munich. None of which interested me in the slightest now that I was immersed in the sights and sounds of Paris. After having lived in the dull English countryside for so many years. I never wanted to see another green field again as long as I lived. I was eighteen years old, and I'd had enough of being forcibly confined in classrooms. It was time for me to start living!

With a life of exciting promise and possibility ahead of me, I looked at the city with new eyes. My taxi rumbled along the cobblestoned streets, jockeying for position with trucks, bicycles, and horse-drawn carts as horns blared and drivers angrily gesticulated at each other. Open-air markets, street vendors and flower stands, cafes and bistros; a magnificent backdrop of elegant, stately buildings…and the Eiffel Tower! Straining my neck to see the top of the tower, I jumped away from the window as an open truckload of grinning faces blocked my view.

French sailors.

Innocent and over-protected as I was, I had no difficulty interpreting the meaning of their catcalls and gestures. Feeling my face flush, I turned away but couldn't help but bask in their admiration, knowing full well how indecent and lecherous they were being. At school, I'd read every smutty book I could get my hands on, including "Lady Chatterley's Lover," but had no real-life experience with boys. Except for with a boy named Arthur I'd met once at the ice-skating rink when I was fourteen. We'd held hands, and then he'd kissed me on the mouth behind the hot drinks' stand. It was awkward because I felt my teeth got in the way, but still, what a great story to tell at school later! Except about the teeth part, of course. It made me feel quite sophisticated.

On a quiet street close to the Jardin du Luxembourg, my mother's house hid behind a six-foot high stone wall and an old-fashioned heavy wooden door. The cobbled courtyard, surrounded by shrubs and small trees, was well-kept. Not that my mother would have deigned to do such dirty work—she must have hired a gardener, I thought as I pushed the ornate brass doorbell.

Miriam, my mother's housekeeper, opened the door with a yelp. Short, plump, and always good-natured, she had worked for my mother for years.

"There you are at last, ma petite!" she cried, pulling me in for a hug. "Your mother isn't here, but someone else is here waiting to see you!" She was speaking in that forced, cheerful tone we all used around Jacques.

There he was, standing hesitantly behind Miriam in the kitchen doorway. He was thinner, I noticed. Taller. His quizzical eyes locked on mine, and for a moment, I felt a stab of pain and thought I might burst into tears. *Don't do that,* I said sternly to myself. *You don't want to set him off.*

"Jacques!" I dropped my bags, crossed the hallway in two strides, and opened my arms to him. As I enveloped him in a hug and stroked his blond curls, he stood stiff and motionless with his arms by his sides.

"It's me, silly! It's Lulu!"

I held him at arm's length to look at him more closely, this boy who would have turned out to be such an intelligent and handsome man if it weren't for me. At first glance, you wouldn't have known anything was wrong with him. The wound on the outside of his head had long since healed. It was on the inside that things weren't right. When you really looked into those blue eyes, you could see the frightened seven-year-old boy trapped inside, unable to move on from what had happened. But I wasn't going to think about that.

"Look how you've grown!" I cried. "You're almost as tall as me now. We're going to have such fun together, you and I, now that I'm home..."

I chattered on mindlessly, then took my bags up to my bedroom and unpacked, quickly throwing my clothes into dresser drawers and the wardrobe. I wasn't planning on staying. My intention was to find a job and move into a shared apartment with some friends. I was sure my mother would secretly be pleased. Oh, she'd likely pretend to object, but not for long. She didn't want me around because I was a reminder.

By the time I went downstairs, she had arrived. Immaculately dressed in a white linen dress with a black collar and cuffs, perfectly applied red lipstick, and not a hair out of place.

"Louise," she said, kissing me on both cheeks.

"Maman," I replied.

"How was your journey?"

"It was so lo-ong," I said, as much for Jacques' benefit as hers. "Taxis and trains and a ferry boat! Then more trains and—"

"Very well," she interrupted. "I see Miriam has prepared us a delicious dinner. We shouldn't let it get cold."

As the three of us sat down at the kitchen table, Miriam said her goodbyes and let herself out. A brief silence descended as we started on Miriam's tasty vegetable soup. I was just about to start talking about how appalling the food had been at school when Maman set down her spoon and looked at me intently.

"I've taken the liberty of reserving you a place at the University in September. To study modern languages. It will guarantee you a job anywhere in the world once you graduate. And you're already fluent in French, German, and English, so I'm sure you'll find it easy enough."

I felt the blood rush to my face.

"No," I said. "That's *not* what I want to do. And you had no right to act on my behalf. I can make my own decisions, thank you very much."

"Indeed! So, what...?" Realizing that she was raising her voice, she glanced over at Jacques and spoke more gently. "Jacques, tuck in your napkin, please. You're dripping soup down your shirt."

We both watched as he did what he was told, carefully tucking his napkin into his collar as if he were a little boy.

"So, what are your plans, if I may ask?"

"I don't know! I'll find a job somewhere, but I'm not going back to school."

"Ah, so you're planning on wasting your life away, are you? Why does that not surprise me? I suggest you do what I ask. You'll thank me for it in the end, mark my words..."

Her lecture went on as we finished our soup and helped ourselves to roast chicken with tiny new potatoes and peas. I had stopped listening, focused as I was on my surroundings. How cozy and colorful the kitchen seemed after the cheerless school dining room. The glow of the polished wooden floor, the glint of shiny copper pans hanging from the ceiling, a golden setting sun peeking through the shutters on the window. A lovely place to live, but I wouldn't be able to stay here. Then my eyes rested on Jacques as he painstakingly pushed his peas into a little pile at the side of his plate.

How could you leave him?

"Don't like peas!" he said, looking over at me with a frown.

I couldn't help but laugh. With surprise, more than anything. He had been completely mute for the first year afterward, but now he would come out with short words and phrases from time to time when we least expected it.

"I went to talk to a new specialist last week," said Maman. "I didn't take Jacques with me this time. If he suspects we're going to the doctor's, he hides under his bed and won't come out. Not that I can blame him after all the poking and prodding that's been done to him these past few years."

She got up to fetch her cigarettes from the dresser. I watched in fascination as she lit up and leaned back elegantly in her chair to exhale.

"I told him—the specialist—the whole story. That he has some sort of brain injury from the fall, but none of the treatments he's had have worked. The doctor is interested in his case but, of course, insists on seeing Jacques in person. I have no idea how I'm going to get him there. Then, of course, there will be the fees. Enough to bankrupt me, let me tell you."

The doorbell rang.

"That will be Joséphine. Let her in, would you? And then you can wash the dishes."

And so it begins. My mother, the dictator.

Joséphine Bernhardt, Miriam's daughter, sometimes came over to babysit Jacques when no one else was home. In exchange for those services, my mother allowed her to practice on the piano that sat otherwise unused in our sitting room. Having completed her first year in music at the Sorbonne, Joséphine was a talented pianist—destined, it was said by her professors, to become a great concert performer.

"Louise!" We kissed each other on the cheeks. "How nice to see you. And now you're home for good! Your mother tells me you'll be joining me at the Sorbonne this fall!"

As she entered the kitchen, Jacques looked up at her and smiled as she ruffled his hair.

"Is it all right for me to practice, Madame?" she asked my mother.

"But of course! You never need to ask; you know that."

As Joséphine went into the sitting room with Jacques following close behind, I started irritably on the dirty dishes, knowing better than to ignore my mother's command. The rich, fluid sounds of Rachmaninoff soon calmed me down, though, and when I peeked into the sitting room, a smiling Jacques was curled up on the sofa with Doudou, his old teddy bear with the missing ear.

A little later, after Joséphine had left, I went to tuck Jacques into bed, wondering if he would remember our song. But I needn't have worried.

"Frère Jacques!" he said as soon as I sat beside him.

The old French nursery rhyme was one that I'd sung to him every night since he was born, from the time when I was just four years old. Except when I was away at school, that is. I used to think it hugely funny that there was a song about my brother Jacques. And he would love hearing it.

Frère Jacques, Frère Jacques,
Dormez-vous? Dormez-vous?
Sonnez les matines! Sonnez les matines!
Ding, dang, dong. Ding, dang, dong.

Now, as I sang, my eyes filled with tears. Here he lay, my brother Jacques, fourteen years old, with the mental capacity of a seven-year-old.

I would never forgive myself.

CHAPTER 4

I'd been home for a couple of weeks, accomplishing nothing more than re-acquainting myself with Paris. Sometimes I would take Jacques to the Jardin du Luxembourg, where he could sail his model sailboat across the lake. Withdrawn and uncommunicative as he usually was, this little outing always brought a smile to his face. As if his troubles were sailing off into the distance on the water in his boat.

I also spent time with my dear friend Emma. She was spending the summer in Paris with her aunt, but in September, she was to return to London to start at a Teachers' Training College with the intent of becoming an art teacher.

I looked at her in horror and disbelief when she told me her plans.

"Ugh, how could you even think about going back to school? God, you'll be spending the rest of your life in classrooms! I couldn't think of anything worse!"

"I have to do something with my life, Lulu," said Emma with a smile. "And I want to get a good job so that I can afford my own apartment one day. I don't want to be living with my parents forever."

"Well, rather you than me," I said. But her words hit home. I needed to find a job so that I could move out of my mother's house.

In the meantime, Emma and I frequented the bars and cafes of the Latin Quarter, along with movie theaters and nightclubs. Which all cost money. I was still using the spending money that my mother had sent me when I was at school but soon realized this wouldn't last forever. The last thing I wanted to do was ask my mother for more money, so I had no choice but to think about a job.

I finally decided to take typing lessons at a local secretarial school.

"There must be hundreds of jobs around for typists," I said to Emma as we sat sipping coffee at our favorite café on the Boulevard St. Michel. "This could be exactly what I'm looking for."

If I expected my mother to be supportive of my decision, I was to be disappointed.

"Typing? That's the best you can come up with?" She threw her hands up in the air in outrage. "Really, Louise, I would have expected better, even of you!"

Determined as I was to prove her wrong, I soon found out that typing wasn't as easy as it looked. I could never remember where the keys were, and my fingers didn't seem strong enough to pound down hard enough or to reach the far edges of the keyboard. After several lessons, I achieved an average speed of fifteen words per minute and started to lose interest.

All the talk at that time was about the threat of war. So many rumors, no one knew what to believe.

"My aunt is terrified that the Germans will invade France," said Emma one night as she was about to leave for England.

"She says that in the Great War, they committed all sorts of atrocities." She leaned forward and lowered her voice. "She says they raped women and killed children!"

I shuddered, trying to block out mental images of such horrific events. "That's not going to happen. Everyone knows that France has a massive army. They wouldn't dare invade here."

But when the subject came up at home, Joséphine told my mother that Hitler was planning to take over the whole of Europe.

"He's already taken Austria. Now he's threatening war with Czechoslovakia. Just last week, he called up 750,000 troops for military exercises. And, of course, he has his eyes on France. I'm terrified—not so much for myself, but for my parents. Any Jews left in Germany have had *everything* taken away from them, and now there are rumors they're being taken from their homes and put in camps. They can't even leave the country anymore!"

For the first time, I realized that Miriam, her husband Aaron, and their daughter Joséphine were Jewish. I just hadn't given that any thought before.

"I'm sure you're safe here," I began. But my words sounded weak, ineffective.

"You know I'll do everything in my power to help if the time comes," said my mother. "Those Nazis will have *me* to deal with if they come anywhere near you or your parents!"

That should be enough to scare them off. I smiled at the thought of my mother standing face-to-face with Hitler, telling him in no uncertain terms to leave the Bernhardts alone.

"Go home, you nasty little man!" she would say in her impeccable German. "We don't want you here!"

As Joséphine closed the door behind her, my mother turned to look at me and shook her head. "I don't know what you think is so funny. This is no laughing matter, Louise. Perhaps you should take a leaf out of Joséphine's book and show an interest in what goes on in the world."

※

By the beginning of September, Emma had left for London, the days were cooler, and I was desperate for some excitement. The glitteringly beautiful Galeries Lafayette department store seemed like the answer to my prayers. With its gloriously domed interior, the store sold everything from haute couture, shoes, and perfume to toys, chocolates, and furniture. It was the perfect place for me to work, I decided, bustling with busyness as it was. The typing lessons weren't going so well; it would certainly be prudent to give up on those.

Much to my delight, I was taken on a position in Ladies Wear on the fifth floor. It pained me that I had to buy a plain black dress to work in, but told myself it would be worth it. All I had to do was to walk around the floor, tidying up here and there as necessary, and provide assistance to the customers.

Mother was incensed.

"So now you're a shopgirl, Louise," she said, lighting up a cigarette then tossing the box of matches angrily across the kitchen table. "A common shopgirl! I'm starting to wonder if you have any brains at all in that head of yours."

I didn't care what she thought.

My first day was exciting. I felt so grown up as I got up early and took the subway to work. For the first hour, with no customers to be seen and under the watchful eye of my supervisor, I ambled around the racks of clothes, caressing the furs and sighing over the silk dresses. After what seemed like an eternity, I was allowed a ten-minute break in the middle of the morning, and by lunchtime, my back was aching, and my feet were killing me in my black-heeled shoes.

"Is it always this quiet?" I asked my supervisor.

"On Mondays, yes," she answered. "It will get busier later in the week."

Six o'clock couldn't come soon enough. Not just on that particular day, either, but for the rest of my time spent working at the Galeries Lafayette.

On the Friday of my first week at work, I arrived home to find my mother waiting for me.

"Ah, there you are at last. Go upstairs and change. They'll be here shortly."

"Who'll be here?"

"I told you last week we're having company for dinner. For heaven's sake, Louise, make an effort for once, would you? Hurry up now!"

Who the company was, I didn't know and didn't care. Probably some of Mother's teaching colleagues, I guessed. Which turned out to be exactly the case.

Coming downstairs, I heard the sound of voices from the dining room. We usually ate in the kitchen, so this must mean that Mother was on a mission to impress someone.

"Louise," said Mother as I entered the room, "you remember Professor Poirier and his wife?"

I did. The couple were old friends of my mother's.

"And this is Tadeus Werner. He's an instructor in German literature at the University. Tadeus, this is my daughter, Louise."

Bespectacled and bearded, he looked every inch a university lecturer. His shirt collar was slightly frayed, his tie was crooked, and his herringbone jacket had definitely seen better days. A little younger than average, perhaps, in his mid-twenties. *Tadeus*, though? What kind of name was that?

"Enchanté," he said, rising awkwardly to his feet and bowing before extending his hand. "I've heard so much about you, Louise." He had a slight German accent. "And I hear you're joining us at the Sorbonne this semester?"

I shot my mother a look of annoyance and sat down without deigning to respond.

Miriam had gone all out with tonight's dinner—boeuf bourguignon with a fresh green salad and her home-baked bread. Jacques was sitting quietly with his head down, focusing on his food. He didn't care too much for strangers, especially men, so he was unlikely to say a word throughout the entire meal. Neither was I, the way the conversation was going.

"When did you move to Paris, Tadeus?" asked the professor.

"Just a few months ago. I was teaching at the University of Berlin and decided to leave mid-way through the semester. It seemed imperative for my parents and I to leave Germany as soon as we could. If we valued our lives, that is. It's not a good time in history to be a Jew, I'm afraid!"

"It must have been terrifying," said the professor's wife.

"It was. The Nazis keep making new antisemitic laws in order to separate us and make us outcasts. As things stand now, Jews in Germany have had their properties and businesses taken away from them and are being denied passports. Even those who were born in Germany!"

As he talked, I wondered vaguely why my mother had invited him. She didn't usually make a habit of including new staff members in her social gatherings. Then it hit me. She was trying to set me up with him, I realized with a jolt, feeling my cheeks turn pink.

A boring conversation about politics followed. What was Czechoslovakia's position, what the British Prime Minister was saying, would Hitler really invade France…the same old talk. I lost interest. When Tadeus politely asked for my opinion at one point, I just shrugged and didn't answer. Churlish of me, I know, but I felt trapped and wanted to escape.

After dessert and coffee, the Poiriers took their leave. Mother said something about helping Jacques get ready for bed, and there I was, alone at the table with Tadeus. He removed his glasses and gave them a polish with his handkerchief before clearing his throat nervously.

"I couldn't help but notice the piano in the other room. Do you play?" he asked.

"Hardly," I said, "but our housekeeper's daughter does."

Possibly out of guilt for my behavior earlier, I found myself telling him about Joséphine and mentioning the beautiful Rachmaninoff concertos that she'd been practicing of late.

Tadeus cleared his throat and tugged at his collar.

"It just so happens that I have two tickets for the symphony orchestra tomorrow. Would you…if you're free, that is…do me the great honor of accompanying me?"

Poor Taddy. He looked so anxious, and he had such kind eyes. I really couldn't turn him down. Especially after having been so rude to him earlier.

"Thank you, Tadeus. I'd be delighted," I said.

I didn't feel so delighted with my mother, though. After our guest had left, I turned on her.

"I know exactly what you're doing. You're trying to marry me off, aren't you? You put me in a very difficult position there. And he's too old for me, anyway."

"I have no idea what you're talking about, Louise," said Mother as she wrapped up the leftover beef to go in the cold cellar. "Such a nice young man, don't you think? And ambitious, too. He'll be a professor in no time with his work ethic. You could do a lot worse than Tadeus."

I could never win an argument with my mother.

Taddy had promised to pick me up at seven o'clock, and I don't think it was a second after or a second before when the doorbell rang. He stood at the front door with a bunch of flowers clutched in both hands, looking as if he were about to faint from fright. He had a taxi waiting for us at the curb and opened the car door for me as if I was royalty. Never in my life had anyone bought me flowers or treated me so politely. It was amusing but also, I had to admit to myself, quite touching.

And I hadn't expected to enjoy the concert as much as I did. Surrounded by elegantly dressed Parisians, I sat back in a plush velvet seat and let the music envelop me. Surreptitiously glancing over at Taddy at one point, I saw him leaning back with his eyes closed. He did have quite a handsome face, I realized. Black curly hair, high cheekbones, dark, soulful eyes.

Good looks aside, I knew he wasn't for me. Once he found out how hopeless I was at everything, he'd soon lose interest. And did he even know that I was just a shopgirl with no plans to attend university? Apparently not. During the ride home in the taxi, I blurted out the question that was bothering me no end.

"Tadeus, I have to ask you this. Did my mother tell you to ask me out?"

He looked at me in amazement with wide eyes for a moment, then threw his head back and laughed as if I'd told an incredibly funny joke.

"Good heavens! No, of course not!"

When he invited me out to dinner the following week, I accepted without hesitation.

CHAPTER 5

My first pay packet, thrilling as it was to receive, didn't go very far after buying new clothes, stockings, and makeup. And the job was starting to bore me. By the beginning of my second week, I felt suffocated by the stuffiness of the air and overly familiar with every single piece of clothing on every rack. Rarely did I see a woman under the age of fifty, and the only men were those in tow with their wives, forced to sit in discomfort at a discreet distance from the changing rooms.

Every day seemed to stretch away into infinity. As my supervisor had informed me, the floor did become busier toward the end of the week, but I soon discovered that the customers didn't particularly want or appreciate my help.

"May I help you, Madame?" I once asked an older lady who was looking at the furs.

A withering stare was cast in my direction.

"Goodness me, no! A chit of a girl like you? I don't think so. Find me someone more *mature* to wait on me, if you please!"

Then there was the time I was assisting a rather large lady in the changing room. She was to attend a cocktail party, she informed me, so needed something glamorous. I brought her a number of evening dresses from the racks in the biggest sizes I could find, and she squeezed herself into a shiny black sequined number, pirouetted in front of the mirror, and asked me what I thought.

"I'm quite taken with it," she said. "I think it will go beautifully with my pearls. What do you think?

The dress was so tightly stretched across her body that the seams would likely split open at any second. In addition, the thin fabric clung to and emphasized every roll of fat. And there were a disturbing number of rolls of fat to be emphasized. I couldn't, in all conscience, allow the woman to buy this dress.

"Umm, perhaps Madame might feel more comfortable in something *looser*?" I suggested.

"Looser?" she said. "*Looser*? What are you implying, girl? Are you saying I'm too big for this dress? Are you saying I'm *fat*?"

Her voice became so strident that my supervisor hurried into the room to find out what was going on. I ended up with a firm warning for my honesty.

"Just remember, the customer is always right!"

Deciding to work until the end of the week so that I could at least collect my pay packet, I spent my lunch hours wandering through the streets in hopes of inspiration, which came sooner than I had hoped.

Bartending Staff Required said the sign outside the Lutetia Hotel. *Apply Within.*

At last, the perfect job.

With my hair done up in an elegant chignon, a thick coating of bright red lipstick, and an intriguingly low-cut blouse that I found at the back of my mother's wardrobe,

I sat across from the manager in his office, determined to prove my worth—a difficult task since I had no bartending experience whatsoever.

"I'm a fast learner," I lied. "I know I'd pick it up in no time."

Monsieur Moreau studied me doubtfully from behind his desk.

"And I can speak German and English in case any of the guests are foreigners."

At this, he suddenly sat up straighter. "That might be an advantage." He paused and looked at me intently. "Wait, though, you're not in sympathy with the Nazis, are you?"

"No!" I answered, surprised by the question.

"The reason I ask, Mademoiselle, is that our bar is a well-known meeting place for German exiles. There is no place here for Nazi sympathizers, you understand."

"Yes, Monsieur, I understand. I'm a hard worker—if you'd give me a chance, I'm sure you wouldn't regret it!"

"Very well," he sighed. "You'll add a bit of ornamentation to the place, anyway." He leaned back in his chair. "I'll take you on for a week to see how you do. But Sacha won't be too pleased to hear he has to train you!"

I was thrilled. The only problem, as I saw it, was that I would have to listen to a load of boring old politics since the place would be full of German exiles. I couldn't seem to escape them, I thought, thinking of Taddy.

I was to start at the Lutetia the following Monday and figured I might as well tell my mother immediately before she found out for herself. She was furious.

"Shopgirl not enough for you? Now you have to sink even lower. *Barmaid?*"

"It will give me more time in the day to spend with Jacques," I said. "And the pay is better. I'll probably earn a lot in tips."

"Money to fritter away in bars and nightclubs, I presume."

"No!" I said, angrily, clenching my fists and feeling my nails digging into my palms. "As a matter of fact, I'm saving up to move out into my own apartment!"

"What?"

We were standing in the front entrance hall. Well aware that Miriam was working in the kitchen and able to hear every word through the open door, I suddenly wished I'd kept my mouth shut. Oh well, too late now.

"You heard me. I'll be moving out as soon as I can. I *know* you don't want me here!"

Stepping back, Mother held onto the banister at the bottom of the stairs as if to steady herself. "Of course I want you here. Why ever would you think otherwise?"

I didn't want to cry, but the tears came anyway. "Because you've *never* wanted me!" I felt myself choking up. "You hate the sight of me! That's why you sent me away to England for all those years. Every time you look at me, you think of my father. I'm to blame. For father, for Jacques, for all of it!"

There. I'd said it to her face. As I ran past her upstairs, she called my name, but I didn't want to hear her deny my accusations. Slamming the door to my room, I cried my heart out wretchedly on my bed, ignoring her knocks on my door. I would make a go of this new job, I determined. Then I would find somewhere else to live.

※

The day after our argument, my mother tried to make amends.

"Louise, we need to discuss this. You have it all wrong."

"No," I said. "I'd rather not talk about it anymore," and I left the room.

On Saturday evening, Taddy, punctual as ever, arrived to take me to dinner, another bunch of flowers in hand, another taxi waiting at the curb. Much as I wanted to fix his tie and smooth down the clump of his hair that was sticking up the top of his head, I resisted.

"I hope you like flowers," he said, giving me one of his old-fashioned bows as he handed them over. "And I hope you don't mind that I've made us a reservation at the Bofinger."

I had no idea what the Bofinger was until Taddy explained it to me on the way there.

"They serve German food like sauerkraut and sausages. It's right next to where the Bastille used to be—and it has a bit of a history itself. It was originally set up for workers from Alsace—that's why they have a German-inspired menu. And, it was the first restaurant in Paris to offer draught beer on tap."

Taddy was evidently pleased with himself for his choice. "I know you're an adventurous soul, so I thought you'd like something different."

He was right. I couldn't help but feel impressed that he understood that side of me.

Over dinner, he told me a little about his upbringing in Berlin, and I told him about my boarding school experiences in England. Then I put him to the test.

"I have no intention of going to the Sorbonne," I said. "I don't want to be a student anymore."

"I understand," he said. "That doesn't surprise me after your terrible time at those boarding schools."

"I've found a job at a hotel. Bartending."

"Really! Which hotel is it?"

When I told him it was the Lutetia, he put down his fork and gasped in amazement as a look of sheer delight appeared on his face. "The Lutetia? How wonderful! I've heard so much about that place and always meant to stop by. It's well-known as a meeting place for exiles and refugees, mostly from Germany. Heinrich Mann apparently goes there all the time!"

By his expression, I presumed I was supposed to know who he was referring to.

"Who?"

"Heinrich Mann! He's a famous writer who spoke out against Hitler in Germany in the early thirties. The Nazis even burned his books. He was lucky to escape!"

"As were you," I said with a smile. "And your dinner's going cold!"

"So it is!" He laughed. "I must be boring you—I'm so sorry. Sometimes I get over-excited about things!"

He wasn't actually boring me in the least, I realized. His enthusiasm was infectious. "Would you mind if I drop in for a beer when you're working there? You never know who I might meet!"

"Not at all! I can practice my beer-pouring skills on you!"

As the evening went on, I found myself talking about all sorts of topics. Even about Jacques. Without giving away my dreadful secret, of course.

"I think it's important for us to get him out in the fresh air as often as we can. He likes to sail his little boat on the lake in the Luxembourg Gardens, but only when it's not too busy. He gets anxious when there are too many people around. I just wish I could think of somewhere else we could go."

On the way home, Taddy surprised me by suggesting that he and I take Jacques to the zoo. "We could go early, so there wouldn't be too many people around. We could even go there by taxi. I think he'd love it!"

I was sure he would, too, so we made plans to go the following day, Sunday.

Seeing the lights still on in the sitting room when I arrived home, I entered the room as Mother put her book down and looked at me questioningly. When I told her about the proposed trip to the zoo, she nodded her head in agreement, and I could see she was trying not to smile.

"So, you and Tadeus are getting along, I presume?"

"Yes," I said defensively. "But that doesn't mean anything."

She stood up and walked over to me, taking my hand and clasping it between both of hers. "Look at me, Louise. I want you to understand something. When I sent you to England, it was for your own good. I thought you'd be happier away from home. I know it's hard for you to be around your brother. So I wanted to spare you the pain."

I looked into her eyes, unable to come up with an answer.

"I know I'm hard on you sometimes. But I see your potential, and it breaks my heart to see you wasting your life away."

I tried to pull my hand away, but she wouldn't let me.

"You're not to blame for what happened, you know. You were *twelve*, dammit, only twelve!"

We both had tears in our eyes, but I couldn't respond. It was too much to deal with. I gave a stiff nod and left the room, taking a deep breath and refusing to let the memories in. After all, I had tomorrow to think about and needed to prepare.

The Zoological Park of Paris was a huge success with Jacques. He pointed, laughed, and, when I prompted him, called the animals by name. Taddy, sensing that Jacques needed space, kept his distance the whole time. His sensitivity and kindness were starting to make a big impression on me.

CHAPTER 6

The Lutetia Hotel was so close to home that I could walk there in fifteen minutes or ride my bicycle in ten. Famous for its magnificent architecture, the hotel was built in an unusual wavy design on the outside, with over two hundred guest rooms inside. How lucky I was to be working in such luxurious surroundings, I thought happily as I entered the marble-floored lobby on my first day.

With wood-paneled walls and deep leather armchairs grouped around polished tables, the bar had the feel of a gentleman's club. The bar itself stretched into infinity down the length of the room, complemented by an intimidating backdrop of mirrored shelves displaying liquor bottles of all colors and sizes. I would have to learn what was in all those bottles, I realized.

Not so happy was the bartender, who eyed me critically as I walked in and introduced myself. Tall and lean, with slicked-back wavy hair, he picked up a spoon from the bar and spun it expertly around his index finger, his eyes never leaving my face.

"So you're my new barmaid. With absolutely no experience in bartending."

"No. But I can speak German and English." I reached for the dish of lemons that was sitting on the bar and started juggling, first with two, then three. A trick I'd learned as a child. "And I can do tricks, too!"

I smiled, and he burst out laughing. "You got me there! Welcome, Louise. I'm Sacha!"

"Call me Lulu," I said.

We shook hands, and I felt like I'd made a friend. I'd come prepared with a small notebook and pencil and made notes as Sacha showed me where everything was. Customers started arriving, and soon I was pouring my first drinks under Sacha's supervision. He was like a dancer, I thought, the way he glided and pirouetted between customers and bottles. After a while, we were joined by a waitress, a flamboyant-looking young woman who introduced herself as Mitzi. With movie-star platinum-blonde hair, fluttery false eyelashes, and a curvaceous figure, I soon saw how popular she was with the male customers.

"Hey, Lulu!" she called to me from down the bar. "I have a customer here for you!"

The customer in question leaned toward me with a hopeful expression on his face as I approached. "Sprechen Sie Deutsch?" he asked. "Do you speak German?"

Delighted to hear that I did, he launched into a detailed description of how he wanted his martini cocktail made.

"The French don't know how to make a good martini, and I just don't have the words!" he explained.

The drink was a success, so much so that the customer gave me a five-franc tip—quite extraordinary since that was my hourly wage. By the end of the night, I had earned an extra twenty francs and accumulated several pages of notes, which I took home to study and learn. I had high hopes of becoming a competent bartender. *Perhaps this is my calling in life*, I thought.

Taddy made an appearance at the bar later in the week. As I served him his beer, he looked around the crowded room. "I think I see someone I know," he said and disappeared from view for half an hour or so before returning for a round of drinks for the table he was sitting at. Every time I glanced over at him, he was deep in conversation with a different person, seemingly having the time of his life.

"Is he your boyfriend?" asked Sacha out of the corner of his mouth as he slid up next to me.

"Oh!" I said. I hadn't previously thought of Taddy as my boyfriend, but surprised myself by thinking that I might like him to be. "Maybe. Well, I suppose so."

"Hm. Interesting," he replied.

"Why? What do you mean, interesting?"

"Well," said Sacha, looking over at Taddy. "He just doesn't seem your type, somehow. I mean, he seems sort of… intellectual."

"Are you saying I'm not clever enough for him?" I laughed and swatted at him with the bar towel, but I knew what he meant.

I myself often had the feeling I wasn't clever enough for Taddy. Regardless, our relationship continued, although with me working at the hotel most evenings, we didn't go out together quite so often anymore. On occasion, when he wasn't teaching, he'd come over and join Jacques and me for a walk to the lake, and sometimes we'd go out for coffee. He apologetically took me to see where he lived, in an old apartment building close to the university that smelled of boiled cabbage. His room was so littered with books and papers I told him I didn't even know how he found a place to sit.

We went to the movie theater and held hands while we watched *La Marseillaise,* a film about the French Revolution. Taddy, always one to analyze everything, said it was made with the intention of arousing patriotism amongst the French people, what with the threat of war looming over our heads and everything.

I started calling him Taddy to his face, sometimes Tad. In retaliation, he called me Lulu, sometimes Lu. Easy to talk to, Taddy never made any demands of me. Never told me what I "needed" to be doing. Most important of all, when I was with him, I felt safe.

Christmas came and went, the first few weeks of 1939 turned into months, and I found myself falling into a routine. I would get up in the morning, after my mother had gone to work, to enjoy a leisurely breakfast of café au lait and croissants while Miriam made Jacques his favorite—poached eggs. If it was too cold or wet to go out, Jacques and I would work on a jigsaw puzzle or play with his toy soldiers or his train set, or if he had one of his headaches, I would put a cold cloth on his forehead and try to distract him with story books.

Miriam always prepared us a delicious lunch of soup and crusty fresh bread or sandwiches, and sometimes in the afternoons, Joséphine would come over to practice on the piano. After Maman had arrived home, I would leave for work. It worked out well for me that I didn't see too much of her, and although I was still saving my wages, it didn't seem so urgent for me to move out.

I tried to ignore, as much as possible, all the rumors and talk of war. For Joséphine, however, it was a topic of supreme importance. She was enraged, affronted, and impassioned over the Nazis' treatment of Jews. On November ninth, there had been an intense wave of violence in Germany, Austria, and Czechoslovakia against Jewish homes, businesses, and synagogues. It had even been given a name: Kristallnacht— night of the broken glass—because of the shards of glass from broken windows that littered the streets.

"They *even* desecrated Jewish cemeteries," said Joséphine, shaking her head in disbelief.

But what disturbed her more than anything else was the insidious antisemitic propaganda Hitler was using.

"They're saying that we're dangerous enemies of the German Reich, that we're subhuman—even making movies to show how evil and depraved we're supposed to be. I don't understand why decent German people don't see what's going on and speak out."

I wondered that too, especially looking at this bright, beautiful, and incredibly talented young woman before me, who just happened to be Jewish herself.

In September, Joséphine was the first to inform us that Hitler's army had invaded Poland, then, a day or so later, that Britain had declared war on Germany. The only way this affected me was that the Lutetia was more popular than ever. For the constant stream of refugees fleeing from the Germans, the hotel was a beacon. It didn't take long for the guest rooms to be full to overflowing with displaced people from Germany and beyond, many of them writers, artists, and musicians.

My mother invited Taddy over to dinner one evening on my day off. It was just the four of us around the kitchen table, enjoying Miriam's famous Coq Au Vin. Now that he was used to Taddy being around, Jacques seemed at ease, and it occurred to me that we seemed like a real family. Once Jacques had finished his chocolate mousse dessert, Mother sent him into the sitting room to play with his tin soldiers.

"I've finally made an appointment with this new head injury specialist I was telling you about," she said. "But Jacques has to be present for the doctor to look at him. Any ideas as to how I can get him there? I haven't mentioned it to him because I know it will send him into one of his episodes."

"Why don't we try bribing him?" Taddy suggested. "We could tell him that all he has to do is let the doctor talk to him and look at his head. And then, if he's good, we'll take him to the zoo straight afterward *and* buy him ice cream!"

Maman thought it might work, and I certainly couldn't think of anything better. A week later, both she and Taddy took the day off from teaching, and we gently ambushed Jacques with an incredible amount of finesse. It worked to perfection. Taddy and I waited outside the doctor's office for forty-five minutes until an anxious-looking Jacques and a thoughtful-looking Maman emerged. As promised, we bundled Jacques straight into a taxi and off to the zoo.

Later on, Maman told me what the specialist had said.

"Shell shock," she said.

"What? I don't understand. Isn't that what soldiers used to get in the Great War?"

"Yes. The doctor says that Jacques' symptoms are similar to what soldiers used to get when they were in battle. Shell shock is the phrase they used to describe it. It's a reaction to the bombs and the fighting—helplessness, panic, fear. An inability to reason, to sleep, or to speak. Nervous shock, I suppose."

I stared at her in amazement.

"The thing is, most of these soldiers didn't have head injuries and hadn't been shot at. He thinks it's an emotional thing. From the shock of seeing…what happened."

I swallowed hard. "All this time, they've been saying it was from his injury," I said. "Can the doctor help him?"

"He will see Jacques again in a few weeks' time. It's a long time to wait, but he's busy, I suppose. He says he's treated similar cases in the past and wants to talk to Jacques to see if he will open up about his father and…what happened. He says he'd like to get to know Jacques a bit more and establish a relationship with him. Then, gradually try to get him to speak about his father. But no treatments. That much he promised!"

My world was turned upside down. To think there might be a glimmer of hope for Jacques, with no treatments, just talk. We had always believed that it was best *not* to talk, that it was best just to try and forget. To leave it all behind us, in the hope that time would heal, in the hope that it would just fade away from memory as if it had never happened. The thought of even suggesting the idea of talking about that day made my head hurt.

But the promised appointment never came to be. Maman was notified by his receptionist that the doctor had closed his office and was unreachable.

☀

In April, the Germans invaded Norway, then in early May, there was a "blitzkrieg" against the Netherlands and Belgium. Thousands of refugees were now escaping the war zones by heading south through Paris. The main thoroughfares were crammed with people in cars, wagons, bicycles, and even on foot.

For me, on my way to and from work, I found it frightening and disturbing to look at; some of them had been walking for hundreds of miles; many looked like they were close to death. I turned away from their desperation and pushed it out of my mind. We were safe enough at home, hidden from view on our side street behind our solid stone wall.

When Taddy arrived unexpectedly one afternoon in June, we sat companionably on the patio with coffee as Jacques lined up his little toy soldiers on the grass.

"I hope that doctor will come back when this is all over," I said. "I really think he might be able to help Jacques."

Without a word, Taddy put his hand over mine and squeezed it gently. I looked at his kind face and suddenly decided I had to tell him. I wanted him to know exactly what had happened on the day my father was murdered. I knew he wouldn't judge me too harshly and thought I'd feel better just for telling him.

Taking a deep breath, I was just about to speak when the door opened, and Joséphine stepped outside. She was ashen.

"I'm sorry, but I thought you'd want to know. France has surrendered to the Nazis. They'll be in Paris by tomorrow."

CHAPTER 7

The refugees were no longer clogging up the streets of Paris on the morning the German army arrived. I held onto Jacques' hand tightly as he, Joséphine, and I stood on the Champs Elysées watching the parade. Although some of the shops were boarded up, the cafes were still open, and people sat on the terraces in complete and utter silence. It didn't seem real. Hundreds of Nazi soldiers goosestepping their way along the boulevard. Tanks, armored cars, and machine guns pointing at us, seemingly ready to mow us down for any indiscretion. Swastika flags everywhere. Tall, fair-haired Aryans, expressions of contempt and superiority on their faces…I suddenly recalled a sight such as this in Munich. But that seemed so long ago now.

Turning to look at the people standing near us, I caught sight of a man with tears running down his face, and a chill ran down my spine. It was as if the French government had betrayed its own people, deciding that it would be better to spare Paris from being devastated rather than to fight back.

As Joséphine explained it to me, the northern part of France, which included Paris, was to be occupied by the Germans, while the southern zone was to be governed by the French.

So Paris had been handed over to Hitler to spare it from being destroyed. Nothing would justify the sacrifice of Paris, said the French government. Not even the lives of its Jewish citizens, apparently.

It was Joséphine who'd wanted me to join her here. Her eyes were red-rimmed from crying—not for herself, but for her parents.

"I begged them to leave Paris," she said, her head down and shoulders slumped. "But they refuse."

"But what about you?" I asked. "Shouldn't you think about leaving, too?"

"Not me," she replied, folding her arms in defiance. "I have to stay and fight!"

Some of the soldiers were throwing bananas and what looked like chocolate bars into the crowd. When Jacques made a move to step forward to pick one up, I pulled him back. "No!" I whispered through gritted teeth. I wasn't the only one refusing to give them the satisfaction of accepting their gifts, I noticed. Most of their offerings lay untouched on the ground.

"Probably poisoned," said a woman behind us.

When the parade finally started to peter out, we started to make our way home to the sound of a German-accented voice making announcements through loudspeakers. A curfew was to be imposed for eight o'clock that evening, it said. How I was supposed to get home after work with a curfew in effect, I had no idea.

Paris was already starting to look unfamiliar. The French tricolor flags had been replaced by huge swastika flags, and German soldiers stood on guard outside public buildings. One of the biggest shocks was seeing an enormous banner spread across the front of the National Assembly building.

"Deutschland Siegt An Allen Fronten!"—Germany is victorious on all fronts!

Even Jacques, who normally seemed unaffected by his surroundings, seemed disturbed.

"Home," he said, tugging at my hand to make me move faster. I didn't need much urging.

⩘

Miriam was apologetic as she served us soup for lunch.

"It's a bit thin," she said. "And I hope the bread isn't stale, but I couldn't get any fresh—all the shops were closed. Even the bakeries."

"It's fine, really," I said. "But should you still be here? In Paris, I mean."

"Of course I should be here! This is my home! Those bullies aren't going to scare me into running away!"

I wondered if she would feel the same way if she'd witnessed the might of their army marching through Paris that morning. The sheer number of them—I couldn't get it out of my head. Where are they all going to live? I wondered.

I was soon to find out.

When I arrived at the hotel later that day, I was shocked to be confronted by an armed German soldier carrying a clipboard as I entered the lobby.

"Halt!" he commanded. "Papers, please!"

"I don't have any papers," I said. "I work here!"

"You work here?" he asked in a heavy German accent. "What is your name?"

"Louise Bellingham."

"Wait here!" He walked over to the reception desk and ran his finger down what was presumably a list of names. "You may enter," he said upon his return. "But next time, you will need identification."

I had no idea what that meant but didn't give it another thought when I became frighteningly aware that the hotel was teeming with Germans. I hadn't even made it as far as the bar when a shout made me freeze in my tracks.

"Halt! Stop!"

I turned around to see one of my favorite customers— Wilhelm, the man who had given me the five-franc tip on my first day. He was heading for the door with a suitcase, which he dropped to the floor in dismay as he was surrounded by soldiers.

"Papers, please!"

I couldn't hear what he said, but saw him fumbling in his inside suit jacket. He showed the German what may have been a passport, which was taken from his hands as the soldier went over to the reception desk and again went through a list of names. I hesitated, wondering if I should go over and tell them that I knew him, that I could vouch for him.

"Take him!" the soldier at the desk suddenly shouted in German. "He's on the list!"

Poor Wilhelm was suddenly grabbed from both sides and marched out of the hotel.

"My suitcase!" I heard him cry.

Another soldier picked up the case and followed its owner outside. I ran to the door and watched in horror as Wilhelm was thrown into the back of a military truck. His suitcase was tossed in behind him, and the truck quickly pulled away.

"Where are they taking him?" I asked in German when the soldier with the clipboard returned.

"He is a Jew. A threat to the German Reich. Why would you care where they are taking him?"

Much to my relief, both Sacha and Mitzi were behind the bar. I looked around to see none of the regulars. The place was practically empty save for a couple of German officers sitting at one of the tables.

"Please tell me I'm dreaming," I said.

"Wish I could," said Sacha. "The Lutetia has been commandeered by the German army. They're taking over most of the rooms and converting some of them into offices."

"Did all the guests leave?" I asked.

"I hope so. Funny thing is, the Boche seem to know who is staying here, and they're trying to track them all down. Saying they're enemies of the Reich or some such rubbish. I'm afraid it's too late for anyone who hasn't escaped by now."

I thought of Taddy, hoping he would be smart enough to stay away from the hotel once he saw all the Germans coming and going. He didn't make an appearance that night, much to my relief, and neither did most of our regulars. We served a few of the officers with drinks, but for the most part, the bar was empty. Meanwhile, filing cabinets, desks, and large boxes were being carried from trucks on the street into the lobby and onto the elevator.

"They're moving in," said Mitzi unnecessarily. It was unnerving, to say the least.

I had forgotten about the curfew until Monsieur Moreau, the manager, brought me a travel permit—an official-looking piece of paper with a Nazi eagle emblem showing my name.

"This is temporary," he told me. "You will have to get a permanent one with your photo, also a work permit, and an ID card."

My stomach dropped. "But…how long will they be here?" I asked. I knew it was a foolish question.

"Oh, not long," I wanted him to say. "I'm sure they'll be gone by the end of the week."

But he just shrugged and shook his head.

My walk home through the empty streets that night seemed unbearably long. Even at this late hour, the streets of Paris should have been alive with the happy sound of couples and groups of friends leaving bars and nightclubs. But tonight, my solitary footsteps echoed across the cobbles as if I was the only person left alive in the whole city. Clutching my temporary permit in my hand, I skulked as close to the buildings as I could, terrified of being stopped, questioned, and thrown into the back of a truck like Wilhelm had been. It was a relief to get home.

⚡

Within days of their arrival, the Nazis were announcing new laws—dozens of them, mostly directed toward Jews. Banned from professions such as the law, medicine, or any type of public service, their businesses were taken over in order to be "Aryanized." Then, incredibly, Jews were banned from cinemas, theaters, public parks, museums, restaurants...and even cafes.

"How can people sit back and allow this to happen?" asked Joséphine.

When I thought it couldn't get any worse, it was proclaimed that Jews could not move without first informing the police. They were forbidden from owning radios or bicycles and could only ride on the last carriage on the Paris Metro trains. *The majority of Jews are illegal immigrants,* said radio and newspaper reports. *They are causing all sorts of social problems and pose a threat to the German Reich and the upstanding citizens of France.*

I hadn't seen or heard from Taddy in almost a week.

"Have you seen him at the University?" I asked my mother.

"No," she replied. "He's not allowed to teach there anymore, remember?"

I had to find him. He would probably be at home, I reasoned, waiting it out. Of course, that's where he is. In my mind, I imagined Jacques, Joséphine, and I standing on the Champs Elysées, watching the German army retreat back the way they'd come. We would throw banana peels and empty chocolate wrappers at them, jeering and clapping. Then I'd go over to Taddy's house. "You can come out now," I'd say. "They've gone!"

Louise, I said, shaking my head at my own stupidity, *you really need to grow up.*

I went over to Taddy's apartment on my bicycle, ran up the stairs, and knocked on his door.

"It's me!" I called. "It's Lulu! Open the door!"

Nothing. Just an empty stillness. I hammered even harder. *Come on, Taddy, you have to be in there. You have to be all right.*

The sound of a door opening down the hall, and I swiveled around to see a woman looking at me. She folded her arms.

"Banging on the door isn't going to make any difference. There's no one there."

"Do you know where he went?" I asked, my voice trembling.

"They took him. In the middle of the night. The Boche."

She disappeared into her apartment, her door slamming shut behind her, as I sank onto the floor in front of Taddy's door. *Not Taddy, no. NO!*

CHAPTER 8

I kept hoping that Taddy would casually walk through the door and be surprised when I told him how worried I'd been. On my way to work, sometimes I would think I'd spotted him in the distance. I'd run as fast as I could to catch up with him, but, of course, it wasn't him at all. I told myself it was the not knowing part that was the hardest.

"Do you think I should ask one of the officers at the hotel if they can track him down for me?" I asked Mother.

"Not unless you want to be arrested yourself," she replied. "We're not even supposed to befriend anyone who's Jewish these days."

And, of course, in all honesty, I knew where he was. We'd heard the rumors about what was happening to foreign Jews. He was a prisoner, being transported to a camp somewhere in Germany. If he hadn't already been shot, that is.

Still, I returned to his apartment time after time over the next couple of weeks, hoping against hope. One day, my heart leaped when the door opened at my knock. It was a complete stranger who'd just moved in. He had no knowledge of Tadeus. "But this is *his* apartment!" I said. "What if he comes back?" "It's my apartment now because I'm paying the rent," said the stranger, closing the door in my face.

I missed him terribly; it was as though there was a hole in my heart. I missed his silly jokes; I missed having him there to hear what had happened at work; I even missed the way he would polish his glasses with his handkerchief when he was nervous. I wanted him back so that I could straighten his tie and smooth down that clump of hair that always stood on end. If I got him back, I would kiss him hard, put my arms around him, and never let him go.

I still took Jacques to the lake with his little boat sometimes, but being out on the streets was dangerous. There were armed German soldiers everywhere, constantly on the lookout for Jews or subversive activity, and incidents of violence were becoming more frequent. On one occasion, I was on my way to work when I noticed a couple of teenage boys pointing and laughing at a small contingent of half a dozen or so soldiers marching down the street.

Oh, no, don't do that! I thought. *This can't end well!*

One of the soldiers noticed the boys and shouted over at them. Within seconds, the boys were being beaten with rifle butts. And when they were bloodied and lying on the ground, they were kicked mercilessly with heavy leather boots. I hurried away from their cries as fast as I could, as did everyone else around me.

It reminded me of a similar incident I'd seen in Munich. At the time, I'd been horrified at the way everyone walked past, as if it wasn't happening. Now, here I was, as guilty as they were. Oh yes, I could tell myself that there'd be no point in me trying to help. That I'd probably get arrested. The truth was that I was scared. *But if you and everyone else did the right thing and faced up to these bullies, this wouldn't be happening, would it, Louise?*

It's something my father always tried to teach me—to stand up to the bullies of the world, especially when they were hurting people weaker than themselves.

Looking up into the distance as I walked, I couldn't help but notice an enormous swastika flag hanging from the top of the Eiffel Tower. *France is ours. We own you,* it seemed to say. *And we're watching your every move.*

∿

At home, Miriam was running low on food supplies. The shops that were still open had empty shelves where the butter and eggs used to be, and as people started panic buying, the shortages became worse. Where the food was going was no mystery—it was being requisitioned by the Germans for their armies in France as well as on the home front in Germany.

"They're taking everything we have," said Miriam. "They're going to bleed us dry."

The next humiliation came in the form of ration books. We weren't allowed to buy anything at all without one, and there was a long list of foods that were rationed, including basics such as bread, milk, eggs, sugar, and potatoes. Our daily rations left us all with hunger pangs, especially since both Maman and I made sure Jacques got extra on his plate.

There were long lines at the butchers and bakeries, and Maman worried about Miriam.

"You're spending hours waiting in line to get food for us. It's not fair—it's not what I pay you for. And I don't want to scare you, but I'm terrified, in case…"

"I know, Madame, I know," said Miriam. "But what would the Boche want with a silly old woman like me? Really, I'm fine."

No one could have done a better job than Miriam at stretching out what little food we had to make it go further. But as the days went by, the thought of food became an obsession for all of us. There was so much to miss. My morning croissant, the fragrant roast dinners that Miriam used to make, not to mention her fluffy omelets. When we ran out of real coffee, we were forced to drink a bitter substitute made from toasted barley and chicory.

And for Jacques, it was even harder because he just didn't understand why he couldn't have an egg every morning. It broke my heart to look at him—already thinner and even more withdrawn. I hadn't forgotten what the specialist had said about how he was planning to get Jacques to open up about Papa. *That's what I should be doing,* I thought. But neither of us had mentioned our father's name since it happened, and much as I tried to summon up the strength to say something, I just couldn't do it.

At least I had my work to help me take my mind off Jacques and my hunger. At first, I'd been afraid that I might lose my job, but when it was discovered I spoke German, I was told to apply for a work permit. The hotel staff had been instructed to answer to Oberleutnant Schmidt, a sour-looking man who addressed us in short, sharp barks as if we were his troops. On one occasion, Mitzi arrived half an hour late for her shift because she couldn't get on a bus.

"I waited for ages, but when one finally came, it was full to overflowing," she said. "I don't know what's happened to all the buses, but I never used to have a problem getting here before."

Oberleutnant Schmidt was unsympathetic, giving her a five-minute lecture in a mixture of both French and German about the importance of punctuality.

"We Germans pride ourselves on our efficiency and punctuality," he barked. "You would be well advised to emulate your conquerors. This is your one and only warning. Next time you will be dismissed!"

With a click of the heels and a "Heil Hitler," he strutted out of the bar, and Mitzi put her head in her hands and sighed.

"Monsieur Moreau would never have shouted at me like that," she said. "Whatever happened to him, anyway?"

Sacha and I exchanged glances. The manager had disappeared from the hotel a few days back. It wasn't too difficult to imagine where he'd gone after all the effort he'd been putting into creating a sanctuary at the hotel for Jews and other exiles with anti-Nazi sentiments.

Now that the Nazis had settled into their living and working quarters at the hotel, the bar became busier. But it was a different atmosphere. In the past, the bar had been seen as a haven for intellectual discussion about art, music, and literature. Voices were intense and passionate but never strident or overbearing. Now, raucous laughter, punctuated by constant Heil Hitler-ing grated irritatingly in my ears. When the Nazis ordered drinks from us, they did so with a contemptuous smile, and when they tipped, they did so as if they were tossing a coin to a beggar. They made a point of making us feel inferior.

"What does 'Heil Hitler' mean, anyway?" asked Mitzi one evening.

"It means 'Hail Hitler' as in 'Hail Caesar,' you numbskull!" said Sacha.

"Yes, but why do they have to say it *all* the time?"

Neither Sacha nor I had an answer for that one.

As the days went by, we got to know some of our customers by name. Most of them were high-ranking officers who'd been billeted to the Lutetia because of the hotel's reputation for luxurious accommodations. But there were also a few enlisted men—in particular, Fritz and Johannes, who would arrive at the bar around ten o'clock every night, taking up the bar stools at one end. Unlike their superior officers, these two joked around with us as if we were equals, becoming louder and friendlier with every beer. Since their French was practically non-existent, they insisted on using me as a translator so that Sacha and Mitzi could understand their jokes, which didn't always translate well, leaving us scratching our heads in confusion.

At least it was a distraction.

It had been almost four weeks since the occupation had started, feeling a lot longer. The weather had turned bitterly cold, and there was no coal or wood to be had. My mother came to the heart-wrenching decision that, in all conscience, she couldn't keep Miriam on.

"You have your own family to worry about," said Mother. "And I don't like the idea of you waiting in queues for hours on end just for us."

There were hugs and tears when she left. Miriam had worked for my mother for many years, and to Jacques and me, she seemed like a member of the family. The following day, it was strange to get up to a cold, empty kitchen. Doing my utmost to sound cheerful, I made Jacques porridge with just a dash of the milk we had left, but he sat staring into space, oblivious to my conversation.

After several attempts to get him to eat, I felt too tired to continue. There was something we had to do today, something that I couldn't put off any longer. It was time to go to the town hall to get our coupon books renewed—a task we had to face every month because the ticket colors changed, apparently to prevent forgeries. It might not have been so bad but for the queue, which could keep people waiting for as long as eight hours. I dreaded it. Jacques couldn't stand in a line of people even for a few minutes, let alone a few hours, especially in the cold.

I bundled him up as best I could and held onto his hand as we headed to the bus stop. The metro would have got us there sooner, but these days, the trains were packed, and Jacques wouldn't have been able to cope. At least the bus had windows.

But when we approached the bus stop, there was a long line of exhausted-looking people. There was no way the bus could take that many on.

"We'll have to walk," I said to Jacques. "It's only three blocks. Come on, now, walk fast so you don't get cold!"

An icy wind bit at our cheeks and made our eyes water. I kept glancing over at Jacques as he slowed down and tried to urge him on. Finally, he came to a complete stop and stared at me sullenly when I pulled at his arm.

We had a block more to go. It seemed hopeless, and I started to cry at the injustice of it all. I was cold, tired, and hungry, and if I didn't get the new ration tickets, we'd end up with nothing to eat.

Something in me snapped.

"*Come on!*" I screamed at him. "*Jacques, you have to keep walking! Do you want us to starve to death? Now, move!*"

I yanked at his arm so violently it must have hurt. His bottom lip started to tremble, but he started walking again, and finally, the end of the queue appeared up ahead. Jacques leaned against the side of the building as we began our wait. His eyes were red, his face pale, and his lips bluish in color. I realized that he hadn't eaten anything today.

"It'll be all right," I said, as much to myself as to Jacques. "Not much longer, now."

But, of course, it *was* much longer. To pass the time and to make up for having shouted at him, I quietly recited nursery rhymes, told stories, and even sang "Frere Jacques" as the line crept slowly forward. By the time we reached the head of the queue, I knew I'd have no energy left to queue up for food at the shops, so we stumbled our way home in a state of utter exhaustion. It was mid-afternoon. I warmed up Jacques' porridge from breakfast which he ate without complaint and took a stale crust of bread for myself. What my mother would feed the two of them for dinner that night, I neither knew nor cared.

All I worried about was summoning up enough energy to get to work later.

CHAPTER 9

"I wish I worked in the hotel restaurant," commented Mitzi as I propped myself up tiredly against the bar. "At least I might be able to smuggle out some food."

"You have to be joking," said Sacha. "With old eagle-eyed Oberleutnant Schmitty in charge? I'll bet he searches everyone before they go home."

"True," Mitzi acknowledged. "But have you seen the food they serve in there? It looks so-o good. Smells good, too. I wonder if the Krauts have to pay for their food?"

"They do," said Sacha. "Same as they pay for their drinks. But the thing is, it's all ridiculously cheap for them. You see, the Germans devalued the franc, so our money is worth next to nothing nowadays."

I felt drained both physically and mentally. Sick and tired of the whole thing. When Fritz and Johannes came in that night at their usual time, I watched them laugh and joke around as I served them their drinks with a forced smile. *When was the last time I laughed?* I wondered. *Or had a bit of fun? So long ago, I could barely remember how it felt.*

Some time after midnight, the pair was joined by a young woman named Lucie.

"She looks familiar," I said to Sacha. "Where do I know her from?"

"From here. The hotel. She's a waitress in the dining room."

Fritz ordered Lucie a martini cocktail, and as I poured the ingredients, Sacha whispered in my ear.

"I think there's some horizontal collaboration going on there!"

My tired brain had no idea what he was talking about. Sacha sighed dramatically and tried again.

"*Collaboration.* With the enemy. *Horizontally!* Get it?"

"O-oh! Now I get it!" As I handed her the cocktail, I decided I wouldn't mind walking in her shoes for a while. She was getting free drinks and having a good time, so why not? Much to my surprise, I *was* actually given the invitation to walk in her shoes.

"After we leave here, we're going to the Normandie. Why don't you come with us? It'll be fun!" asked Fritz.

The Normandie was a nightclub I'd heard of but never visited. I hesitated for just a moment.

"Come on, where's the harm? I got paid today, so the drinks are on me!" Fritz insisted. He had a nice smile, I noticed. "We'll leave when your shift ends!"

I accepted his offer, hoping that Sacha or Mitzi hadn't overheard. Not that I was doing anything wrong, I told myself. I just didn't want to be judged or accused of collaborating. Not that there would be any collaboration on my part. Horizontal or otherwise.

For the rest of the night, I acted as casually as I could and, when we were about to close, leaned across the bar to quietly tell Fritz I'd meet them at the hotel entrance. But if I thought I was going to slip out with them unnoticed, I had another thing coming.

"See you out front, Lulu!" shouted Lucie in French, at full volume, as they slid off their bar stools. I swiveled my head around to see if my co-workers had heard, but of course they had. Mitzi was gazing at me with a puzzled expression while Sacha folded his arms, frowned, shook his head, and then looked away as if to say, "I thought better of you."

The four of us tumbled into a taxi, and I soon realized that Lucie didn't speak German. With Fritz and Johannes not able to speak French, I wondered how they'd been communicating all this time. But it didn't seem to matter. Each of them would speak loudly and slowly in their own language—as if we were all deaf—while performing incomprehensible mimes. There was a great deal of laughter, but it didn't seem to matter what anyone was saying, especially after all the drinks they'd had.

The taxi pulled up a few minutes later outside the nightclub, the sound of swing music spilling out onto the street. Inside, it was dimly lit, loud, and smoky. We stood at the bar, and I asked for a martini because that's what Lucie was having, and I didn't know what else to order. I danced and drank and smoked Fritz's cigarettes, then danced some more until the room started to spin, and I could hardly stand anymore. I remember sitting at a table and resting my head on my hands, but I think I must have passed out because when I woke up, the club was starting to empty.

"Ah, Lulu!" said Fritz. "It's four o'clock, time to go. Do you want to come back to the hotel with me?"

Inebriated as I was, I knew what was on his mind. I struggled to remember what Sacha had said to me earlier about sleeping with the enemy, but I couldn't recall the words he had used.

"No," I said, "I need to go home."

"If that's what you want," he said. Befuddled and bleary, I was led to a waiting taxi; I gave my address to the driver and was soon dropped off outside the house. Whether or not I thanked Fritz for the evening, I have no idea, but I did know enough to creep inside so as not to wake Maman. Lying down on my bed without changing out of my clothes, I gripped the sides as the room spun tipsily around me. *You're going to have a heck of a hangover tomorrow, Lulu,* I thought.

A heck of a hangover, indeed. It was Saturday, so Maman was home, although I had to go to work later. My head was throbbing painfully, and my mouth was dry as a desert when I finally made it downstairs.

"Good Lord, Louise, you look terrible," said Maman. "Are you sickening for something?"

"I don't know. Maybe," I mumbled, thankful at least that I hadn't woken her up when I'd come in at the crack of dawn.

"I'm going out to see what I can get in the way of bread," she said. "So you can stay and look after Jacques, all right?"

I shrugged. "It's what I do *every* day, in case you hadn't noticed."

Jacques was sitting at the kitchen table, staring into space. I had no energy to try and coax him out of his trance. As soon as Maman left the house, I ignored him and went back upstairs to lie on my bed in the hopes of sleeping it off, finally managing to drift into an uneasy doze. *Never again,* I thought. *I will never, ever drink alcohol again.*

Arriving at the bar later that day, I knew I'd have to answer to Sacha.

"Good Lord, Lulu, you look terrible," he said as soon as he set eyes on me. "Did we have a drink or two too many?"

"Not that it's any of your business," I said irritably, "but yes, as a matter of fact, I did. Happy now, are you?"

He pursed his lips and frowned at me suspiciously.

"And just so you know, there was no *collaboration* of any kind! Just drinks. And dancing. That's it."

"Fine," he said. "But just be careful, will you? Don't get too friendly with them—remember who they are."

"*I know, I know!* They're the enemy. I get it. But *I'm* not French, you know. I wasn't born here. This isn't actually my war!"

When I saw his face, I knew I'd gone too far and regretted my outburst. I was about to apologize when Mitzi came over.

"Lulu! You look terrible!" she said.

"Oh, for heavens' sake," I said. "I wish you'd all keep your opinions to yourselves!"

The bar was busy, it being a Saturday night, and the rest of the shift felt awkward as both Sacha and Mitzi tried to stay out of my way. Not that I blamed them. But the more I thought about what they'd said, the angrier I became. *I'm fed up with people telling me what to do all the time,* I thought. *I can do what I want.*

When Fritz and Johannes showed up, I made a point of going straight over to them and being friendly, well aware of Sacha's disapproval. Then, Fritz asked if I wanted to go out with them again that night.

"After last night? I don't think so!" I said. "I've never been so hungover!"

"Hey, who said anything about drinking?" said Fritz. "We're going to get a light supper at a cabaret. Come on, it'll be fun, and it *is* Saturday! Lucie's coming too!"

I didn't care about the cabaret, the fact that it was Saturday, or even that Lucie was going too. All that caught my attention was the word "supper." It was unthinkable to turn down the chance of food. And when the bar was closed down for the night, I made no attempt to hide the fact that I was going out with my new friends.

As on the previous night, we went to the club in a taxi, and the two Germans paid for everything. Remembering what Sacha had said about the French franc being devalued, I knew that it wasn't actually costing them that much, so I didn't feel the least bit guilty. We sat at a table, sipping on champagne and eating what tasted like the most delicious food I'd ever had in my life. As the singers and dancers performed on the floor in the center of the room, a waiter brought us small savory pastries, cold meat, olives, cheese, bread, strawberries…I couldn't focus on the performers.

Fritz and Johannes seemed almost unaware of the food, tasting it occasionally without much reaction. And no wonder. They would have eaten their fill at dinner at the hotel earlier. Desperately wanting to smuggle some of it out for Jacques, I deftly wrapped up a small parcel in my handkerchief and slid it into my handbag under the table. It was a trick I'd learned at boarding school when I was younger—the only difference being that, back then, it was to remove the inedible food that I was supposed to eat from my plate for future disposal.

Then I saw that Lucie, who was sitting right beside me, was watching.

"It's for my brother," I said in French, knowing that the Germans wouldn't understand what I was saying.

She flapped her hand at me as if to say that she understood.

"Can you take food home from the hotel restaurant?" I asked out of curiosity.

"Honestly, I think they'd have you shot if they thought you were stealing food. But there are ways!" she said, with a wink and a smile. "Johannes, cigarette, please?"

The word "cigarette" was the same in both languages. Johannes understood and was all too pleased to offer his cigarettes around.

This is the life for me, I decided, leaning back on my chair to enjoy the show. *And I don't care what anyone else thinks!*

CHAPTER 10

I got into the habit of going out with Fritz, Johannes, and Lucie on Fridays and Saturdays and occasionally during the week, too. Maman never caught on to the fact that I was coming in just before sunrise, and I could always take a nap during the day if I felt the need to catch up on my sleep. We went to nightclubs and cabarets all over Paris, sometimes eating, sometimes dancing, but always drinking. We had nothing in common, the four of us, but we enjoyed each others' company and laughed a lot about nothing. For me, it was just the escape I needed.

Sacha made a point of showing his disapproval, but I didn't care.

"Life's too short," I would say to him. "I'm just having a bit of fun, after all. Don't be so hard on me!"

Fritz sometimes gave me packs of cigarettes and chocolate bars. He would kiss me goodnight and always asked hopefully if I would go to his room with him, but that wasn't something I was ready for. Not because he was the "enemy," but because I didn't have strong feelings for him. He was good company and fun to be around, but for me, nothing more.

The chocolate bars I would give to Jacques. When Mother asked where they had come from, I told her they had been given to me at work as a tip.

"Ask if they could give you a loaf of bread next time, would you?" she said.

I knew she was joking, but the idea of asking Fritz for food had occurred to me. He seemed like a kind-hearted person, so I was sure he would be willing to help.

But the opportunity never came. Fritz and Johannes suddenly stopped coming to the bar. And when I sought out Lucie in the restaurant to ask if she'd seen them, she shook her head.

"No, they haven't eaten here in two days," she said. "I suppose the army must have sent them somewhere else."

"That's a shame," I said. "We always had such a good time together."

She nodded sadly. "I really liked Johannes, and I think he liked me too. I don't understand how he could just leave without even saying goodbye."

As for me, I had no strong feelings for Fritz. He was nothing compared to Taddy. All I cared about was how I could survive without my nights out.

"*I hate this country, and I hate this war,*" I wrote to my friend Emma in England. Her reply, which took a month to make its way across the Channel, was unsympathetic.

"*At least you're not being bombed all the time,*" she wrote. "*Not only are we starving, but we have to spend most of our nights in bomb shelters. Or the Underground. I'd give anything to have your life right now.*"

⟍⟋

With November came cold winds and never-ending torrential rain. As the shortages became even more acute, we found ourselves in even longer queues. On one occasion, I stood for an hour outside the bakery, only to get close to the front of the line to see the owner pull down the shutters and close up because he had nothing left to sell. We ran out of soap and were having to use a substitute that had been made by one of Mother's colleagues at work. Made from fat and caustic soda, it smelled awful.

"Just be grateful," said Maman. "I had to give up a packet of cigarettes for that bar of soap."

Stockings were impossible to find, as were leather shoes—or anything made of leather, for that matter. Apparently, it was all being requisitioned by the German army to make boots. Jacques, having outgrown his old shoes, had to wear wooden clogs that rubbed his toes and made them sore. Not that he needed shoes very often anymore. He rarely left the house.

Jacques was starting to have nightmares again. At least once or twice a week, I'd be woken up in the middle of the night by his cries. Mother would always tend to him, going into his room and speaking to him gently, sometimes even singing him a lullaby. Sometimes I thought about how fortunate he was to be unaware of what was going on. Every few days, we'd hear more upsetting news, most of which was relayed to us by Joséphine.

The latest news involved a twenty-eight-year-old Frenchman who had been coming home from his friend's wedding. He and his companions ran into a group of German soldiers, a brawl broke out, and one of the Germans was punched. His friends escaped, but the man was arrested and refused to give up their names. He was charged with "an act of violence against a member of the German Army," taken to court, and sentenced to death.

"He was shot by firing squad," said Joséphine. "This is what we are dealing with now."

I put the story out of my mind; refused to think about it. What I was thinking about was the safest way of smuggling a bottle of champagne out of the hotel bar.

On one particularly bleak November morning, as I chopped up some turnips for soup, I felt more than usually depressed. I hated turnips—had always hated them—and the watery, lumpy soup we were forced to eat nauseated me. The kitchen was freezing cold. Bursts of rain were hitting the windows like little pebbles, and Jacques was rocking himself back and forth in his chair.

I couldn't take it anymore. I had to get out, if only for a little while. Without Jacques.

Finishing up with the turnips, I put them into a pan, filled it up with water, and set it on the stove to heat up. Then I went and put on my coat and knelt down in front of Jacques.

"I'm going out for a bit, but I'll be back soon." He made no sign that he'd even heard me. "Just be good, all right? Play with your soldiers or something."

As I approached the door, I turned back to look at him in a pang of guilt, but he didn't seem aware that I was leaving. I wasn't supposed to leave him. We'd never left him on his own, ever since...*But what's the difference?* I reasoned. *He doesn't know if I'm here or not!*

I was wet through within minutes of leaving the house, but I walked quickly. I knew exactly where I wanted to go, and it wasn't far. The Boulevard St. Michel. That vibrant, bustling street with wide sidewalks and so many cafes to choose from. I would go to my favorite—the one that Taddy and I loved so much. I would sip my hot coffee, devour a croissant still warm from the oven, and watch well-dressed Parisians as they saunter along the street.

But, of course, it didn't happen that way.

The boulevard no longer bustled. There were hardly any cars on the roads anymore. Why would there be when there was no more gasoline to be had? Most of the cafés were boarded up. The place that Taddy and I had loved so much was unwelcoming, dimly lit, with only sour-looking Nazis sitting at the tables. And as for well-dressed Parisians? They didn't exist anymore. Parisians were worn-out, weary, more worried about where their next meal was coming from than how they looked.

Why would I think that nothing would have changed?

Sick at heart, I headed home with my head down against the wind, flinching as icy drops of rain hit my face. Relieved to be inside at last, I closed the front door, took off my coat, and shook the excess water away.

"Jacques!" I called. "I'm back!"

No response, of course, so I headed into the sitting room. Empty. As was the kitchen and the dining room. *He must be in his bedroom*, I decided, running up the stairs.

"Jacques! Where are you?"

He wasn't in his bedroom, or mine, or Mother's. I ran back to his room to look under the bed, but nothing there.

Oh, no, what have I done? I left him alone, and now he's gone.

Hurriedly, I dashed back downstairs to look in the pantry, the cold cellar, behind the sofa.

"Jacques!" I sobbed.

I stood at a loss in the dining room. Then it happened. Without any warning, like a tidal wave, the memories overcame me. As I sank to my knees, I was back in time, back in our old apartment, shouting his name, begging him to come to me.

It had been a normal afternoon, like every other. Jacques and I had come home from school and were sitting at the dining room table doing our homework. Maman wouldn't be home for another hour while Papa was in his study down the hall with his door open so that, as he used to say, he could hear what we were up to.

That's when it happened.

Someone knocked on the door to the apartment. Excited to see who it might be, I ran to open the door, forgetting that I wasn't supposed to. We always had to look through the peephole first, Maman said. If it's someone we don't know, we don't open the door.

But I did. I opened the door.

Two men with scarves tied around their faces and guns in their hands pushed by me and stepped into the apartment. As the door banged shut behind them, my father must have realized something was wrong.

"Lulu? What's happening?"

One of the men grabbed my arm and pushed me into the dining room. Then there were muffled shouts. As I stood frozen with fear, Jacques ran out of the dining room.

"No! Jacques, come back!" I shouted. Still, I didn't move. I was glued to the spot. Paralyzed by fear.

Then a loud bang. I knew it was a gunshot because I'd seen their guns. I saw the men dash past the dining room door on their way out and heard them open the front door, which slammed shut behind them. And when I crept along the hallway into the study, shivering in abject terror, I saw two bodies on the floor. My father had been shot dead, and my brother was unconscious from a knock to the head, probably resulting from him falling or being pushed into the corner of a side table.

The police never arrested anyone for my father's murder, but they believed it was related to his position at the British Embassy. One theory was that it was Indian revolutionaries to blame, wanting revenge for Britain's colonization of India. Which made no sense to me. My father had nothing to do with that.

On that day, our lives changed forever. Jacques was unconscious only for a few hours, but when he woke up, he was a shell of the boy he used to be. And here we were, ten years later, after countless visits to doctors, seeing no improvement.

Pulling my thoughts back to the present, I realized where I was, sitting on the floor of the dining room. *He must have left the house*, I thought. *I need to get my coat on and go look for him.* But as I got to my feet, he was suddenly there, standing in the doorway, looking at me.

"Thank heavens you're here. Where were you?" I asked, tears coursing down my face as I enveloped him in a hug.

He didn't answer me, and even though I searched the house again later, I didn't find his hiding place.

But that afternoon, I pulled a well-worn book from the shelf and showed it to him.

"How about a story? I asked, swallowing hard. "Winnie the Pooh. Do you remember when Papa used to read this one to us?"

I held my breath and watched his face for a reaction. A slight frown, then his eyes met mine and slid away. Quickly I turned to the first page and began to read aloud.

It was a start, anyway.

CHAPTER 11

Joséphine had come over to the house to practice. On her way out, she told Maman and me that she was helping to plan a demonstration against the occupation. Students from the University were going to gather together on November eleventh, the anniversary of the end of the Great War, at the Tomb of the Unknown Soldier under the Arc de Triomphe.

"Usually, on November eleventh, we have ceremonies of remembrance, but the Germans won't allow it this year," she explained. "I think it's important that we make our voices heard. They have no right to take Armistice Day away from us."

She looked at me, and I knew she was going to ask me to join in. Every fiber of my being screamed, "No." *In case you didn't know, I was born in Switzerland*, I wanted to say. *That makes me neutral. It's not my war.*

"Louise, I know you're not a student, but would you join us? The more people we get, the better."

The passion and determination in those dark eyes of hers left me no leg to stand on. Not to mention the fact that my mother was also standing there awaiting my response. "Yes, I'll come," I said. I wanted to ask her if she knew how dangerous it would be, but didn't bother. Of course she knew. "Then it's settled," said Maman. "I'll leave work early and make an appearance there myself on my way home. I'll be back in plenty of time for you to head over there before you go to work, Louise. It would be no place for Jacques, that's for sure."

"Thank you," said Joséphine. "Now I have to go out and spread the word!" She pulled a pile of handwritten notes out of her bag and passed one over to me.

"*November 11, 1918 was the day of a great victory—November 11, 1940 will signal an even greater one!*" it read.

A victory for whom? I asked myself. There were *thousands* of armed soldiers in Paris. How could a handful of students even hope to make a difference?

But it turned out to be more than a handful.

∿

When Maman came through the door early, as promised, on the afternoon of November eleventh, I was disappointed. I'd hoped that she'd arrive too late for me to attend the demonstration since I had to be at work by six o'clock.

"I went over to the demonstration to see how things were going," she said as she took off her coat. "And you won't believe it, but there are hundreds of people there! Such a turnout!"

As I left the house, I considered my options. If Maman was right, and there were hundreds of people there, there was no need for me to go. I could say that I looked for Joséphine but couldn't find her amongst all the crowds. Then again, it wasn't as if I had anything else to do. Although there was the threat of rain, it was fairly mild out. And I'd be riding my bicycle along the Champs-Élysées, which might provide some distraction.

By the time I approached the Arc de Triomphe—it must have been close to five o'clock by that time—I heard the roar of a crowd. But not just a crowd. *Thousands* of people were milling around the Arc, fists in the air as they shouted at the soldiers that surrounded them. Some of them were running toward German trucks, throwing stones, and that's when the shooting started.

The first shot was fired, and I couldn't bear to watch. Turning my bicycle around, I retreated as fast as I could, hardly able to see the road through my tears. Once I arrived at the hotel, I went straight to the ladies' room and splashed cold water on my face, then tried to behave as if nothing had happened. I wasn't going to even think about the possibility of Joséphine being killed. *Or should I say, murdered.*

Sacha knew me well enough to realize that I was upset about something.

"Missing our little German soldier, are we?" he asked smugly. "Or is it that there's no more champagne and chocolates!"

I ignored him, pretending to be more interested in collecting the dirty glasses and trying my best to also ignore the conversation that was going on at the bar between two Nazi officers. That was the trouble with knowing German—I understood every word they said, even when I'd prefer not to.

"A demonstration! How pathetic!" said one. "What do they think they can achieve, these French? Other than their own annihilation, that is!"

"I have to agree," said his colleague. "Birdbrains, all of them! Isn't that right, bartender?"

As Sacha—not understanding their words—smiled at them questioningly, the pair erupted into raucous laughter, slamming their beer mugs onto the counter in delight. Just at that moment, I looked up in disbelief to see my mother and Jacques heading toward me. *Oh no,* I thought. *She's come to tell me about Joséphine.*

"Thank God you're here," she whispered. "I had to come and make sure you escaped."

"Yes, I'm here," I said weakly. "What about Joséphine?"

"She was arrested, that much we know. They've taken over a hundred students to the Cherche-Midi Military Prison, apparently."

"Did anyone…was anyone killed?" I asked.

"No. The shots were fired into the air." She looked around nervously. "I don't know how you can work here with all these…Never mind, we should go. I just had to make sure."

I breathed a sigh of relief but then thought about Joséphine in prison and shuddered.

※

Within a couple of days, the event was making headlines in the newspapers. It was said that between three and ten thousand people from all walks of life attended the demonstration. A hundred and fifty students had been arrested, and some had received prison sentences. As for Joséphine, she was released the morning after her arrest, which I thought was fortunate until I heard what happened to her.

She never mentioned it herself and acted as if nothing untoward had happened, but Maman knew otherwise, having heard the story from another student who was also arrested.

"They were slapped and stripped, then they were made to stand outside in the courtyard—in the rain—for hours overnight," Maman told me.

I looked away in horror, not wanting to know anymore.

"Wait, there's more."

I wanted to put my fingers in my ears.

"They were led to believe they were going to be shot and were lined up facing the prison wall. The soldiers shot their guns into the air and laughed. Then they were allowed to leave."

As further punishment, the University was closed down for a month, all students had to report regularly to the police, and there was an increased military presence around the streets of the Sorbonne. And now, at least for a month, Maman had no job to go to, so she was home all day.

⋇

"It's intolerable," Joséphine said to us a few days later. "I can't sit back and allow this to go on anymore."

Her eyes looked haunted. She was thinner, paler, but full of fire.

"They're stealing our food and our art, burning our books, taking our jobs away, and renaming our buildings. People disappear—all the time!"

I thought longingly of Taddy.

"We have to fight back! While we still have the strength to do so. Before they starve or beat us to death!"

I didn't want to hear anymore. *What was she going to ask me to do now?*

"I've been talking to someone who thinks we should get organized. For my part, I want to set up an underground newspaper. And there are other suggestions. Cutting phone lines, disabling trucks—that sort of thing."

My mother intervened. "You know what will happen to you if you get caught?"

"Of course I do!"

Of course she does. She knows better than anyone.

"Count me in," said Maman. "Should we set up a meeting with your friend?

"Yes, that would be the first step."

"Well, let's have the first meeting here. I'm more than happy to do what I can to bring those bastards down. You're absolutely right. It's time for us to fight back."

I looked at my mother in disbelief. Disbelief that she would put the lives of both Jacques and me at risk. But then, she had never backed down from a fight, I realized. Secretly plotting to overthrow the Nazis would be right up her alley.

Later that day, I discovered her avidly listening to the radio in the sitting room.

"Louise!" she said, turning around quickly in surprise. "For heaven's sake, don't creep up on me like that!"

"What are you doing?" I asked.

"Listening to the radio, of course!" she snapped. "What does it look like?" Then she lowered her voice as if we were surrounded by spies. "It's BBC Radio London!"

She was tuned into the radio station that the Nazis had banned everyone from listening to because it encouraged us to rise up against the occupation.

"I know, I know it's *verboten*," she said when she saw my expression. "But it's the only way for us to find out the truth about what's really happening in the rest of the world. Makes a change from all the German propaganda and lies, let me tell you!"

It was as if my mother had a new purpose in life. And at first, I was grateful because it took her attention away from me. Now she had other people to boss around.

The meeting took place a few days later at three o'clock in the afternoon. A total of five people sat around our kitchen table, including Maman. I knew Maman's friend, Professor Poirier, and I knew Joséphine, of course, but I'd never set eyes on the other two. One of them was a man with a beard that was starting to turn gray and a scar over one eye, the other was an athletic-looking young man, possibly a student.

"Come along, Louise, sit yourself down," said Maman impatiently.

"But what about Jacques?" I asked. I had presumed I'd be looking after him rather than being involved in the meeting.

"He's listening to music on the radio in the sitting room. He's fine."

As I took my seat, the man with the beard introduced himself.

"I'm Claude. This is André, and I believe the rest of you know each other. No last names or other information, please. It's important we know as little as possible about each other."

Claude had a tough, no-nonsense attitude about him. As I looked at his weathered face, I wondered if he'd been a soldier and had perhaps fought in other wars.

"Before we begin, I want to make something perfectly clear. Our business here is dangerous but vital. We are on a mission to uphold our honor and do everything in our power to undermine the enemy. But if you wish to participate, you must vow to live quietly so as not to attract any attention. Is that clear?"

So, Claude here is obviously taking charge, I thought.

"It's not like we have any choice but to live quietly," I said with a laugh. "I mean, what is there to do these days?"

I meant it as a joke to lighten the atmosphere, but all I got was frowned at and ignored.

"Our biggest disadvantage is that we have no weapons," Claude continued. "But we have our wits, and if we plan carefully, there are many ways in which we can hurt them."

The others seemed intent on his every word as he went on about the importance of secrecy. We should go about our normal routines, never do anything out of the ordinary that might arouse suspicion, and never, under any circumstances, talk about what we were doing here. To anyone.

I stifled a yawn and wished he'd stop talking. *Nothing but rules and regulations. Don't do this, don't do that.* It was just like being in school. As Joséphine talked about her plans for a newspaper, my stomach growled with hunger, and my thoughts drifted toward what we could make for dinner.

"Isn't that right, Louise? Louise!"

"Sorry, what?"

"I was telling Claude about your work permit and your travel pass. You're the only person I know that's allowed to be out after curfew!"

"I'm sure that will come in very useful, Louise!" said Claude with a smile.

I gave him a forced smile in return. I didn't want to be "useful," particularly at night.

I had other plans.

CHAPTER 12

There were to be no more secret meetings at the house, much to my relief. Claude said they were too risky. He said he'd contact each of us directly if we were needed. As the days went by without us hearing from him, I began to feel a little more hopeful that nothing would come of it. But I wasn't exactly off the hook. Maman had volunteered to take charge of setting up the underground newspaper, informing me that I was to contribute a couple of articles.

"I don't know why you're pulling such a face," said Maman. "It's not like you have anything else to do during the day."

"I do have things to do, actually," I said. "I look after Jacques, for one thing."

That much was true. I was making an effort to get him to read and to do some arithmetic every day. And I was artfully bringing Papa's name into the conversation as often as I could. So far, with not much of a reaction, but I didn't want to push him too far.

"What am I supposed to write about?" I asked miserably. Writing—any kind of writing—had not been my strong point at school, and I had no idea where to begin.

"Just a paragraph or two about the V sign to start. Encourage people to join in."

I sighed. We'd learned about the V sign from BBC Radio. The letter V, for victory, was appearing on walls everywhere, driving the Germans to distraction.

"I should think everyone knows what the V sign is by now," I grumbled. "Seems a bit pointless to me."

My mother pursed her lips and raised her eyebrows at me. I knew better than to keep talking.

As Christmas approached, the food situation became dire. The shops all had tantalizing displays in their front windows—labeled "fake," just in case anyone actually believed they were real. We queued up for hours but rarely had the opportunity to get meat, potatoes, sugar, milk, or eggs. Swedes, turnips, and cabbages were often all we came home with.

My mother did everything in her power to make sure Jacques didn't go hungry, even risking everything by using the black market. She knew someone at the university, she told me, who was making trips into the countryside to buy milk and eggs from the farms. Only trouble was the prices were exorbitant, and the threat of being caught was all too real. There were posters everywhere that left us in no doubt as to what would happen to anyone caught buying or selling in the black market. With an image of two sinister-looking figures clandestinely exchanging a loaf of bread for money, the caption read:

Black Market: A Crime Against the Community

And in the background of the picture, hanging threateningly over the men's heads, was a noose. We all got the message loud and clear.

In exchange for some of her old jewelry, Maman managed to obtain a rabbit for our Christmas dinner, along with some eggs and flour. Those eggs lasted a long time—no more poached eggs for Jacques. Instead, we mixed one egg with water and cornstarch to make an omelet to feed the three of us. Oddly enough, we were still able to get cigarettes with our tobacco allowances, and there was no shortage of wine.

On Christmas morning, we exchanged gifts. Jacques' eyes lit up when he saw his new set of miniature cars and a model airplane kit. I gave Maman a gold cigarette lighter that I had found in an antique shop. I thought it suited her because it was so elegant, and it still worked, too. Meanwhile, she surprised me by giving me one of her old cocktail dresses that she had re-made to fit me. Made from black silk, it was almost ankle length, with a wide, off-the-shoulder neckline.

"I don't know when you'll have an occasion to wear something like this," she said sadly. "But I'm sure that day will come. Eventually."

"It's beautiful, thank you!" I said. I knew exactly when I was going to wear it, but wasn't about to tell her. She most definitely would not have approved.

That night, we ate sparingly of the rabbit, with the intention of making soup from the leftover bones. Carrots and cabbage accompanied the meat, and Maman had made dumplings from the black market flour. It was more than we usually got to eat but nowhere near enough to make us feel full.

"Do you remember the turkey that Miriam cooked...?"

"*Don't*, Louise," said my mother sharply with a frown. "You're just going to make us all hungrier. Keep your thoughts to yourself!"

I did as she asked, but food seemed to be always uppermost on my mind. Also on my mind was New Year's Eve. Lucie and I were going out on the town!

The thought had occurred to me one night at work. Why shouldn't Lucie and I go out together one night? We both had permits that allowed us to be out after curfew. We could go to one of the nightclubs we used to go to with Fritz and Johannes and mingle with the soldiers. If we were clever enough, we could get all our drinks paid for! Lucie was all in favor and came up with the suggestion of going on New Year's Eve.

"The clubs will be more crowded then. We could pretend that we were with our German boyfriends but that we had lost sight of them. We don't want anyone thinking that we're on the mooch!"

We arranged to meet after I'd finished my shift at the hotel. I was elated. For once, I had something to look forward to. I carefully folded up my new silk dress and took it with me to work to change into afterward, and did my utmost to put on a sad face so that Sacha wouldn't catch on to the fact that I was going out.

He saw right through me.

"Why is your hair done up so extravagantly tonight?" he asked suspiciously. "And what's with all the makeup?"

"Just making an effort, that's all," I replied nonchalantly. "It *is* New Year's Eve, in case you haven't noticed."

"Hmm," he said with a sideways grin. "I *know* you're up to something!"

The bar was packed with Germans that night, all looking so pleased with themselves, loudly toasting the Fuhrer and the Fatherland with the finest champagne, especially when the clock turned twelve.

"To the new age of Aryan rule!" called a loud voice across the room.

At least I was on the receiving end of a few tips that night. Not that the money was much use, though. There was nothing in the shops for me to spend it on.

Lucie and I had decided to go to the Normandie nightclub, which was where we'd been once before with Fritz and Johannes. It was close enough to the hotel that we could walk there, and we felt safer going somewhere we were familiar with. Also, Lucie said we could probably get in through the back door without paying.

As we walked arm-in-arm along the frosty streets, I complained to Lucie about my mother.

"She treats me like a child! I'm so sick of it. I'm going to move out—find an apartment with some other girls, maybe."

"Really?" asked Lucie. "We have an extra bedroom in our apartment, my sister and I. The room is small, mind you. If you like, I could talk to my sister to see if she'd be willing to let you move in."

My heart leaped. How perfect. "Yes, please!" I said. "That would be wonderful!"

Arriving at the club, we slipped inside through the back door as planned, carefully hiding our coats in a storage room. The place was packed with Germans, some, although not all, with female companions. The music was loud, and the air thick with smoke.

We knew exactly what to do.

Standing near the bar with anxious expressions on our faces, we pretended to scan the room as if we were looking for someone. Plenty of men looked our way, so I knew it wouldn't be long before one of them took it upon himself to rescue us. *Hopefully with champagne*, I thought, trying to keep a straight face.

"May I be of assistance to you young ladies?" asked a booming voice in heavily German-accented French.

Our would-be rescuer must have been close to seventy years old. Bald, with an enormous paunch, he stuck a cigar in his mouth and looked us up and down appreciatively.

I glanced over at Lucie, and she looked back at me in dismay.

"No, thank you," I said. "We're just waiting for someone!"

"Indeed?" he asked heartily. "Then *someone* should be ashamed of keeping two such beautiful ladies waiting. Come with me. I insist. You will be my guests until your friend arrives!"

"But…"

"No buts! I give the orders around here! General Klaus Hartmann, at your service!" He clicked his heels and gave a slight bow. "Heil Hitler!" Smiling broadly to reveal crooked brown teeth, he extended his arms and herded us toward a table.

Just as I was about to sit down, I yelped in shock as he smacked my rear end. I was about to give him a piece of my mind, but he held up his hand to stop me.

"Forgive me, Mademoiselle. French women bring out the *beast* in me!"

I was about to tell him I wasn't French and didn't appreciate being manhandled, but thought better of it when I saw all the stripes, ribbons, and insignias decorating his uniform. It wouldn't be wise to start telling a Nazi general what you thought of him. He sat Lucie and me on either side of him, calling loudly for more glasses and more champagne, and I realized we had become the center of attention, seated as we were at a table of high-ranking officers.

The champagne was good, but the General's sweaty hand was on my knee while his other hand was on Lucie's. To the amusement and appreciation of his colleagues, not realizing that I could understand German, he joked about how warm his bed would be that night. He refilled our glasses, then put his arm around me and pulled me in close.

"How about a dance, meine Liebchen?"

He breathed heavily into my ear, and I gagged at the fetid smell of his breath. This could be our chance to escape, I realized.

"Of course," I said. "But first, I have to powder my nose! Excuse me, please."

I didn't have to tell Lucie to come with me. She instantly stood up and followed me as the General called after us.

"Hurry up, Liebchen!"

We did as he asked. Grabbing our coats and exiting through the back door into the cold air, we looked at each other and shrieked with laughter as we ran.

"Eeuuw! So *disgusting!* Thank God we managed to escape!" said Lucie.

"Not exactly the night we were hoping for, was it?" I asked. "Never mind, we can try again another time!"

After a block, we split up and went our separate ways home. In spite of it being New Year's Eve, there were few cars and even fewer people about because of the curfew. I still had a good distance to go when I was suddenly blinded by an intense spotlight.

"Halt! Don't move, or we will shoot. Put your hands in the air!"

I did as I was asked. I knew it was one of the German patrols, and I knew that I had the right papers, but even so, I was instantly rigid with fear. In this dark, lonely street, anything could happen. I stood frozen in the bright light for what felt like minutes, unable to see anyone behind the light.

With a start, I wondered if the General had sent out a search party for Lucie and me. After all, we had made a fool out of him by not returning to the table.

"Where are your papers?"

I fished my documents out of my handbag as the beam was lowered, and a young soldier approached.

"Why are you out after curfew?" he asked, taking the papers from my hand.

I decided it might be in my best interest to speak German. "I was working," I answered. "At the Lutetia Hotel. In the bar. And now I'm going home."

The soldier shone his light in my face again.

"Are you German?" he asked incredulously.

"No, I'm Swiss," I answered. *Neutral,* I added, but only in my head. *So leave me alone!*

"Very well," he said. "You may go."

As he handed back my papers, I realized that if he knew the whereabouts of the Lucretia in relation to where I lived, he would have known I was way off track.

"Thank you," I said as I walked briskly away, breathing a sigh of relief. "And Happy New Year!"

CHAPTER 13

On New Year's Day, we were all supposed to stay indoors between three and four o'clock in the afternoon to listen to Radio London as a show of what they called "passive resistance." It wouldn't have made much difference to me, as I'm sure I would have been home anyway, but then the Germans made a ploy to take us away from our radios by offering us free potatoes. When I heard a loudspeaker in the distance announcing that the potatoes were available at the Rue Mouffetard Market, I defied my mother and went off on my bicycle.

We hadn't had potatoes in months; I was heartily sick of turnips and didn't care how angry she would be. And apparently, I wasn't the only one to show weakness—there was a fairly lengthy queue when I arrived. *At least I have the satisfaction of knowing that I'm not French*, I thought self-righteously. *Unlike the rest of the people here.*

Once I was home, I wordlessly put the potatoes on the kitchen counter and waited for Maman to unleash her rage.

"Whose side are you actually on, Louise?" she asked coldly. "Because, honestly, I'm starting to wonder."

"They're for *Jacques!*" I responded angrily. Which was partly true. "Now, if you'll excuse me, I have an article to write!"

I left the kitchen, slammed the door behind me, full of self-righteousness, and went to the sitting room to try and compose an article about the V sign. But all I could think about was the possibility of moving out to Lucie's apartment. It was exactly what I wanted. But what about Jacques? I was the one who looked after him during the day when Maman was at work. Then there was the problem of the food rationing. If I moved out, he and Maman would certainly end up with less food.

I sat there miserably, chewing the end of my pencil until the front doorbell rang. I heard a man's voice, then my mother came into the room with Claude.

Could this day get any worse? I wondered. *Come to think of it, could my entire life get any worse?*

"Louise!" he said. The dark circles under his eyes made me wonder if he'd been partying the night before. He didn't look like the partying type, I decided, imagining him sitting and drinking alone. "You're not working tonight, I believe. It's your night off."

How did he know that? Maman, of course!

"We need your help."

I was about to tell him I had other plans when the doorbell rang again. It was Joséphine.

"Did you ask her yet?" she asked as she entered the room.

"No, I was just about to," said Claude.

The way Claude and Joséphine described it, you would think it was an innocuous little adventure that was so simple and easy to pull off, it would be over within minutes. The Jeu de Paume was an art gallery that the Nazis had taken over as a place to store their stolen plunder, which included masterpieces from the collections of French Jewish families like the Rothschilds. According to Joséphine, these works of art were being shipped to Germany, where they would be divided up between Hitler and a high-ranking Nazi by the name of Hermann Göring, who was in charge of the operation.

"They're planning to take away several truckloads from the Jeu de Paume tomorrow morning," said Joséphine. "Andre and I are going to sneak over there tonight and disable as many trucks as we can. Even if it just means slashing their tires."

My heart sank.

"But what do you need me for?"

"We want you to stand guard. If you see anyone coming, signal us with your flashlight, and we'll know to run. Then you walk away, and if they stop you, it'll be no big deal because you have your papers."

No big deal, she says.

I thought about it. I *had* been stopped on New Year's Eve, and it hadn't turned out so badly.

"You do realize that this won't stop them, don't you?" I asked. "The Germans will have those tires replaced within hours."

"Yes, I know that," said Joséphine pleadingly. "But we want to put up a fight. Show them that we're not all rolling over!"

I could never have lived with myself if I were to turn her down; unhappily, I agreed. What lay heavily on my mind was the fact that the Germans had made it quite clear that there would be no mercy granted to anyone engaging in sabotage and that all saboteurs would be shot. Over the last three months, there had been at least half a dozen Frenchmen shot. The Nazis seemed to take great pleasure in making the public aware of these executions, hoping they would act as a deterrent.

Trouble was, with people like Joséphine and Claude, rather than being deterred, they became even more determined. It was on the tip of my tongue to tell them that I would help them just this once and never again, but it would have sounded ill-mannered. Not to mention cowardly. So, it was arranged for me to meet them at the Jeu de Paume at midnight. I was to wear dark clothing, carry a flashlight, be sure to have my papers with me, and not be late. Most importantly, if any Germans were to approach, I should never, under any circumstances, run. I should walk toward them, showing no sign of guilt.

As the day wore on, I became increasingly uneasy. If I were to be stopped and questioned close to the Jeu de Paume, how could that not arouse suspicion? Located in the Tuileries Gardens, I'd have a hard time explaining why I was in a park on my own at midnight. Added to that, if they took the time to check, they'd discover I wasn't even working tonight. And if I followed Joséphine's advice and dressed in dark clothes, that would surely make me look even more suspicious.

I made the decision to dress in my usual work clothes and coat, which was, unfortunately, a light beige color, and set out from home far too early—a big mistake because I had to keep walking so as not to loiter. The Germans didn't like to see anyone loiter. By the time I caught sight of Joséphine and André approaching the park, my hands and feet were frozen. Without a word, I followed them at a distance and watched as they climbed a chain link fence that enclosed the trucks. Trying desperately to stay calm, I walked up and down outside the perimeter of the fence, praying for it to be all over.

Please hurry up, I kept thinking.

Then, *crash!*

I instinctively jumped away as something on the inside of the enclosure hurled itself at the fence and howled at me. A mass of fur and fangs, not three feet away, desperately trying to tear down the fence with its claws in its desire to tear me to shreds.

A dog! They have guard dogs!

In the distance, a flashlight appeared, and the sounds of shouting were drowned out by the dog's barks.

I did the only thing I could. I ran. As fast as I could, away from the park toward home. I ran until my lungs started burning, and I was gasping for breath and didn't stop until I reached the relative safety of our street. *Damn you, Claude,* I thought, bending over to ease the cramps in my legs. *Shouldn't you have checked everything out before sending us out on a suicide mission? Dogs! Of course they'd have dogs! Even I should have realized that.*

Now I'd gone and deserted Joséphine and André by doing exactly what I'd been told not to do. I'd run away. And I hadn't even warned them—but how could I when I was about to be attacked by a beast of a dog?

With a glance behind me to make sure the German army wasn't on my heels, I let myself into the house. I hadn't even taken off my coat when Maman appeared.

"How did it go?" she asked, then noticed my tear-stained face. "What happened?"

"There was a dog," I said. My hands were trembling, whether from cold or fear. I didn't know. "I ran away. I had to. I had no choice."

Maman looked away from me for a second, put her hands up to her face, then turned back to look at me.

"So you left them there?"

"I told you; I had no choice. I would have been attacked by this massive dog!"

"All right. We'll just have to hope for the best, then." She shrugged and turned to go upstairs, but my inner rage and sense of injustice couldn't allow her to leave.

"I'm moving out!" I blurted.

She turned back to face me, narrowing her eyes. "Moving out? Where will you go? And what about Jacques?"

"What about Jacques? I can't look after him for the rest of my life, Maman. I'm nearly twenty-one! I want a life of my own!"

I'd wanted to hurt her, and by the look on her face, I'd done just that. So why did I feel so wretched?

"If that's what you wish, Louise, then I can't stop you."

She turned her back on me and went upstairs, leaving me feeling heartsick and guilty; my coat still on and my hands still shaking.

∿

Every time I closed my eyes that night, I saw the German Shepherd's sharp, glistening fangs, picturing Joséphine and André lying on the cold, hard ground surrounded by soldiers with guns. The more I told myself that I'd had no other choice but to turn and run, the more unsure I became.

I should have stayed, I said to myself finally. *I should have stopped where I was, faced up to the guards, and pretended to be an innocent passerby.*

Really? Another voice said. *Do you not think you would have been taken in for questioning in the park at that hour of the night?*

When I got up, Maman was sitting in the kitchen smoking, watching Jacques as he ate his porridge. I'd forgotten that it was still holiday time, and she wouldn't go back to work for another few days.

"There's coffee left," she said without looking at me.

I wanted to apologize; for what, I didn't really know, but just then, the doorbell rang, and she hurried to the door.

"Come in, come in," I heard her say. "Are you all right?"

It was Joséphine, putting her hand to her heart when she saw me.

"Thank goodness you're here, Louise! I was so worried about you! What happened?"

I told my story about the dog and the shouts; it sounded lame. The more I tried to explain how terrified I'd been, the less believable it became. After all, the dog had been on the other side of the fence.

"I'm sorry," I said, finally. "I let you down."

But of course, Joséphine wouldn't hear of it. "No, no, you didn't let us down in the least! As soon as we heard the dog barking, we ran. And we did manage to cut a few tires!"

She stayed to practice on the piano. No more soothing Rachmaninoff, however. Her choices now included Tchaikovsky and Beethoven—difficult, fast-paced, and intense pieces that seemed perfectly suited to her agitated frame of mind. As she played and Jacques curled up on the sofa to listen to her, I cornered Maman in the kitchen.

"I meant what I said last night. About moving out. But I'll come over every afternoon to play with Jacques or to take him to the park."

"Very well," she said. "I can see you've made up your mind. But you know he can't be left on his own. I'll have to see if Miriam will come over in the mornings to watch him."

That afternoon, I took Jacques to the lake with his boat, anxious to ask Lucie if her offer of a room was still standing.

Meanwhile, my mother and I barely exchanged a word for the rest of the day.

CHAPTER 14

Before starting work behind the bar that night, I went into the restaurant to find Lucie.

"Did you ask your sister about me?"

"Yes!" she said. "She's fine with you moving in as long as you pay a third of the rent!"

Lucie agreed to come to the bar after her shift, so we could talk more. Finally, my life was about to change for the better. Free at last. Well, as free as I or anyone could possibly be in German-occupied Paris.

A lighter, happier me worked through the first two hours of my shift until a particularly loud German voice caught my attention. *Why did it sound so familiar?* Looking along the bar to locate the face behind the voice, I stood riveted to the spot as my eyes rested on the last person I would ever wish to meet again.

The General. General Klaus Hartmann, to be precise. The cigar-smoking, bottom-smacking, lecherous old man from New Year's Eve. The one Lucie and I had run out on. This was a disaster—I couldn't let him see me! Scurrying up to the opposite end of the bar from where he stood, I kept my face turned away and tried to look natural. Which wasn't easy, especially with eagle-eyed Sacha at hand.

"Louise, what are you *doing*, exactly? There are customers down at the other end that need serving!"

"I know! But I can't go down there, or he might see me!"

"*Who* might see you?"

"The General! If he recognizes me, I'm dead. He'll have me shot!"

Sacha laughed. "Oh, good heavens, Lulu, take a five-minute break if you must. But no longer, mind. It's busy tonight!"

I breathed a sigh of relief, about to leave the bar, when, out of the corner of my eye, I saw someone heading in my direction.

"Hello, Lulu! Can you take a break with me for a few minutes?"

It was a smiling Lucie! If the General saw the two of us together, he'd be sure to recognize us. Without thinking, I ducked down behind the bar.

"It's him!" I said in a stage whisper.

"What?"

She leaned over the counter to peer down at me. "Have you lost your mind?"

"No! Look to your right. Down the bar. It's the General from New Year's Eve!"

As she looked, I stood up and also looked. And the General looked back.

"Go!" I called as I ducked down again. Her face disappeared from view, and I sat myself down on the sticky floor for what seemed like minutes. Finally, without taking the risk of checking to see if he was still there, I got up and walked briskly to the exit, keeping my face averted.

Lucie was waiting for me outside the ladies' room. Once inside, we fell over each other, laughing so hard that we cried. "Did he see us?" we kept asking each other. "Do you think he recognized us?"

Eventually, we calmed down enough to arrange that I should go and see her apartment the following morning. Cautiously making my way back to the bar, I saw no sign of the General and smiled to myself as I thought about what fun it was being with Lucie. We were two of a kind. Moving in with her would change my life.

⋇

In the meantime, I was still expected to accompany Joséphine and André on some of their sabotage missions. Once or twice a week, I would meet them at a prearranged spot—being careful never to loiter—and I would follow them at a discreet distance, acting as a lookout. On these missions, they were painting the V sign on walls and tearing down posters. I realized they needed me because of my permits, but still, I couldn't help but feel resentful at having to walk the streets of Paris after my shift at the bar. It was cold, my feet hurt, and my heart wasn't in it. Truth be told, I was also scared.

"Just remember, if you spot any patrols, flash your light in our direction to warn us. But don't run. Walk toward them as if you have nothing to hide," said Joséphine. I knew she was thinking about what had happened with the dog.

"Isn't there anyone else you can ask?" I boldly asked on one occasion. But the look on Joséphine's face—of disappointment and anxiety—made me wish I'd never opened my mouth.

She was about the same age as Lucie and I, but so different. I couldn't possibly imagine *her* sneaking into a nightclub and trying to get free drinks out of the German soldiers. That would be unthinkable for Joséphine. All her effort and energy seemed to go into these acts of sabotage against the Germans. Then again, it was much more her war than mine, I realized, especially since she was Jewish.

Thankfully, we didn't encounter any patrols on those outings. I had hoped that after a while, there wouldn't be any walls or posters left untouched, so our work would be done. It didn't quite work out that way, though. Claude soon decided it was time to take things up to the next level.

He surprised me one afternoon when I was home alone with Jacques. The doorbell rang, and he slipped inside as soon as I opened it without so much as a greeting.

"Are you alone?" he asked as we stood in the front hall.

"Yes, except for Jacques," I said.

"There are a couple more jobs I need you to help us with," he said. "But from now on, you'll be notified at the bar where you work."

I looked at him in dismay. "What do you mean?"

"There's a hidden slot just under the bar at the end farthest from the door. You can feel it with your hand if you reach underneath. That's where you'll find the messages that are intended for you."

"What kind of messages?"

"All you'll see is a place name and a time, telling you where and when to join up with us. That's it. If the message is ever found, no one would ever think anything of it."

I swallowed hard. "Listen, I…I really don't think I'm cut out for this sort of thing. I think you might be better off finding someone else."

His face softened. "I get it," he said. "But you're all I've got right now until I can find someone else. You have a perfect alibi for being out at night; that's what makes you so valuable.

I don't want to tell you any more than I have to, but what we're about to do will save lives. That's how important it is!"

I nodded despondently.

"When you go to the bar tonight, you'll find a blank piece of paper in the slot. I want you to take it out, tear it in half, and put it back again, all right? That will let me know you've found the slot."

"Very well," I said, impatient for him to leave. I just wished they'd leave me alone.

Later that day, I found the slot under the bar, exactly as described. As instructed, I removed the blank sheet of paper, ripped it in half, and replaced it when I was sure no one was watching. The back of my neck tingled as I wondered who had put it there in the first place. It had to be someone who worked at the hotel.

For the rest of the night, I watched Sacha and Mitzi curiously. Could either of them be involved? Maybe I didn't know them as well as I thought I did.

∖∣∕

I settled into my new home almost immediately. Lucie's apartment was on the fifth floor of an old building with few modern conveniences, and it was further away from the hotel than I would have liked. But I didn't care. I rode my bike to work and felt deliciously grown up to be living away from my mother for the first time in my life. My bedroom was cramped, with barely enough room for the ancient bed and dresser it held, but it was mine.

Since Lucie's older sister Marie worked during the day, our paths rarely crossed, but she made a point of making me feel welcome.

"We only have one firm rule," she said when I first arrived. "We don't bring men back to the apartment. Other than that, we have a rota for cleaning and shopping, but that's it!"

I couldn't have been happier. Lucie and I would chatter away to each other endlessly, often doing the shopping together so that the time spent queueing went a lot faster. And I ate a little better than I had done at home. Lucie would often bring food home with her from the restaurant—very *verboten*, of course. She showed me the deep pockets she had hidden in the inside of her skirt, perfect for a few slices of bread, pastries, and even the odd steak or sausage.

I kept my promise of going home every afternoon to spend time with Jacques until Maman came home, and Lucie even came with me sometimes for a short visit until she had to leave for her shift at the restaurant.

On one occasion, we even managed to arrange our days off to coincide and went to the movie theater together to see *The Last of the Six*, a mystery thriller that, for two whole hours, transported us to another time and place where there was no such thing as a war going on. It brought back memories of the last time I'd been to the movies with Taddy.

On the way home, I told her all about Taddy. Lucie listened sympathetically.

"That must be so hard for you. I still miss Johannes. I was really falling for him. I know it's wrong because he's supposed to be the enemy, but really, he's just a man—a good man, too."

"We can't help the way we feel, can we?"

"No," she said, her eyes shiny with tears. "It's probably for the best that he's gone. If my sister had found out I was going out with a German soldier, she'd have killed me!"

Since we were sharing so much, I wanted to tell her about my unwilling participation in the Resistance but held back. I hoped that soon I'd be able to wriggle out of it somehow. And Lucie wasn't even aware of the times that I was out so late, so it wasn't as if I had to explain my absence.

If it weren't for the war, life would have been practically perfect.

CHAPTER 15

As the weeks went by, we began to take the occupation for granted. The swastika flags, which in the beginning had seemed so offensive, were now an everyday part of the landscape. And the enemy—the soldiers we saw every day, became familiar faces. It was an unspoken rule amongst Parisians that we should ignore the Germans as we passed them by, as if to say that, to us, they were invisible and certainly not worth being acknowledged.

For myself, working at the bar, and indeed for Lucie, working in the restaurant. However, we weren't at liberty to ignore them, for that would have lost us our jobs. They may have been Nazis, but of course, like every other nationality, there were both good and bad among them.

Speaking of bad, we both became constantly plagued by the presence of the General, who, we realized, must have been living at the hotel. Like all the other Nazi guests, he ate his meals in the restaurant, much to Lucie's distress.

"He watches me all the time," she complained. "I'm terrified that he remembers me! If I'm ever asked to serve at his table, I don't know what I'll do!"

"He stares at you because he's disgusting and depraved, and he's not going to recognize you in your waitress uniform," I said. "Don't forget, it was really dark in the nightclub." But I knew how she felt. On occasion, he would sit at the bar and stare at me, too. "And anyway, if he recognized either of us, don't you think he'd say something?"

"You're right, he would," she agreed. "Best not let him see us together, though. That might trigger his memory!"

On my part, I asked Sacha to serve the General when he came in. I didn't want to take the chance of standing directly in front of the man if I could help it.

"Do I get to know the reason why you're so scared of the General?" asked Sacha. "Or do I just have to do it because you say so?"

"You know very well the answer to that question!" I answered with a smile. Sacha might bite my head off with his scorching sarcasm, but underneath, he had a kind heart and always looked out for me.

I religiously checked the secret slot every night and was relieved to find it empty for two straight weeks. Then, out of the blue, came the next summons.

Pont Saint-Michel, 1.

From this cryptic note, I deduced that I was supposed to meet someone at the Saint-Michel bridge at one o'clock after my shift. It was an annoyance because it had been raining all day. I considered not showing up—pretending I didn't get the message, but couldn't bear the thought of all the recriminations I'd be sure to get from Maman and Claude, not to mention the reproachful looks I was sure to receive from Joséphine.

I wondered who had put the note there. Mitzi certainly didn't seem the type…but Sacha? I was sure he was capable of keeping secrets. And as for anyone else, there was the cleaning lady I saw on a regular basis. She mopped her way around the bar, the restaurant, and the lobby. A number of waiters and waitresses could come behind the bar, too, for a bottle of wine, glasses, or ice. It could have been anyone.

I set off on my bicycle for the bridge at a quarter to one, cursing Claude every inch of the way because it was raining steadily. I was wearing my raincoat and had a scarf on my head, but felt cold and wet through within minutes. I shouldn't be out in these dark, deserted streets on my own; it was dangerous. Claude would have to find someone else whether he liked it or not.

Arriving at the bridge, I dismounted, wondering if I should cross to the other side. But a figure emerged from the shadows with a soft whistle, and André was talking at me in a low, urgent tone before I could even get my bearings.

"I didn't hear you," I said, interrupting him. "You'll have to say that again."

"A truck is about to arrive. We have to unload…we have to take what's in there onto the barge below. Understand?"

"Yes." I nodded.

"Your job is to look out for patrols. If you see one, signal us with your flashlight, and walk toward them. You must distract them. For as long as you can."

"I suppose so," I said.

"Just keep them as far away as you can. *Please*, we're depending on you!"

I nodded again, and he disappeared into the darkness. I wheeled my bike onto the bridge and looked down at the river. Sure enough, a barge was sitting there, half hidden by the bridge itself. For a moment, all I could hear was water lapping against the boat, then the sound of an engine in the distance. As the truck slowly approached and pulled up beside the bridge, I saw that its headlights were off.

Then, a flurry of silent activity. The back doors of the truck were opened, and I could make out Claude and André lifting something down. But, no, it wasn't a something. It was a some*one*. Someone in white bandages who'd been injured and was being supported on either side by Claude and André as they helped him down the steep stone steps to the embankment below.

I stood in the middle of the road with my bicycle, looking behind me and in front of me for approaching headlights. *Please hurry, please hurry,* I chanted, stamping my feet on the ground to try and keep them warm.

But it didn't take long. The doors were closed, the truck drove off, and a low whistle from the steps made me turn my head.

"Go! Go!" called a voice, and I didn't need to be told again.

If I hadn't realized it before, I knew now that I was part of a large-scale operation. I'd heard about the Resistance on the BBC News and from newspapers, and I knew that there were groups of resisters not just in Paris but all over France. What had taken place tonight must have required a great deal of planning and organizing, and the wounded man being taken away on the barge may have been a British soldier or a Jew evading capture. I would never know who he was and didn't wish to find out.

And I didn't want to take part in such an operation again. The problem was that I didn't know how to get in touch with Claude to tell him. *And this time, I am going to tell him,* I promised myself. *I'm not asking. I'm telling.* Out of desperation, I wrote a note for the secret slot before I could be summoned to the next job.

Count me out.

Loud and clear—how could anyone not understand that?

∗

What I did want was more fun in my life. The next morning, I suggested to Lucie that we go to a nightclub the following weekend.

"What?" she said, looking at me incredulously with her hands on her hips. "You want to go back to the Normandie? After what happened with the General?"

"Well, maybe not the Normandie. Somewhere else. Oh, come on, it'll be fun! We can at least try for some free drinks. And you never know who we might meet!"

She didn't take much convincing, and the following Saturday night, we left the hotel just before one o'clock for Le Caveau—on our bicycles. Fortunately, it wasn't raining. Taxi cabs were almost impossible to come by, and it was too far for us to walk, so it had to be the bikes.

"What's the point of doing up your hair and looking nice when you have to go out on your bike?" I grumbled. "I really, really hate this war."

Le Caveau turned out to be as loud, smoky, and crowded as every other club we'd been to. We paid to go in because we couldn't find a back door to sneak in by, and stuck to our usual routine, standing helplessly near the bar as if waiting for someone.

"Buy you two ladies a drink?" asked a slightly swaying figure dressed in the familiar Nazi uniform. He was young, good-looking, with the all-too-common blond hair and blue eyes.

He had asked in German, so I pretended not to understand him.

"Ah, French. *Drink?*" he asked loudly. His eyes were bloodshot, and his words slurred.

"No, thank you," I said. "We're waiting for someone."

Lucie nudged my arm. "What did you say that for?" she asked in a whisper.

"Well, I don't want us to seem *too* eager," I whispered back.

The soldier stumbled his way back to a table, and from the looks we were getting from the other occupants, it looked like we were being talked about. After a couple of minutes, another soldier got up from the table amidst gales of laughter from the others and headed our way.

This one, a little older than his friend, perhaps, stood in front of us, clicked his heels, said a "Heil Hitler," and bowed.

"Please forgive my ignorant friend," he said. "He has no manners. My name is Heinrich. Please allow me to buy you a drink."

I tried to look unsure.

"Champagne!" he said. "The finest bottle of champagne!"

Within a couple of minutes, we were seated at their table, once again the center of attention as the men vied for our attention in their awkwardly flawed French over the loud music. Most of the time, I had no idea what they were trying to say. But we drank, we danced, and we laughed, reminding me of the good times we'd had with Fritz and Johannes. I endured a few uncomfortable dances with Heinrich, who kept pulling me too close with insistently wandering hands, and every time I looked around for Lucie, I saw her dancing with the same soldier. The way they were smiling at each other made me wonder if she'd found someone to replace her beloved Johannes.

The drinking was non-stop. After a while, a couple of the soldiers were slumped over the table, and the others were shouting over the music, spilling their drinks, and toasting the Fatherland. And I was starting to get a headache.

"I think I'm hungover already," I said to Lucie when she came back to the table. "We should go. Don't forget we have to cycle home!"

"Just a minute," she said, going over to her dance partner to say her goodbyes.

As we started to leave, Heinrich objected.

"Nein, nein, you must not go! Another bottle! Wait here!" he said, heading over to the bar before I could tell him no.

"Come on," I said to Lucie. "Now's our chance to escape!"

As we left the table, I picked up the almost empty bottle of champagne. *No point in wasting it,* I thought, deciding to put it in my bicycle basket.

The cold, fresh air instantly revived me as we went around the side of the building to retrieve our bicycles. It was a narrow alleyway, almost pitch black, but for the moonlight. I had unlocked my bicycle chain and was about to wheel my bike out of the alleyway with Lucie behind me when a figure appeared out of the darkness and blocked my path.

"Where are you going?"

It was Heinrich, sounding strident, accusatory, angry.

"It's late. We're going home," I replied, trying to get around him.

"Oh, no, you don't," he said. He was speaking German now. "You owe me for all the champagne I bought for you! I'll take my payment now!"

He lunged drunkenly toward me and wrapped me in an aggressive hug, trying to kiss my mouth. Squirming away in revulsion, I let go of my bike and, as it fell to the ground, gave him an almighty shove. Something hit my foot—the champagne bottle. Wondering briefly if there would be anything left inside, I bent down to pick it up.

"You French whore!" Heinrich growled. "You'll do exactly what you're told!"

He grabbed me painfully by the hair at the back of my head with one hand and yanked up my skirt with the other. Lucie screamed. As she tried to pull him off me, he let go of my skirt for a second and pushed her to the ground. Then he was unbuckling his belt, and I couldn't get away from the fierce grip he had on my hair.

But I still had the bottle in my free hand.

Crack!

For a moment, he was slumped heavily over me. I stepped away, giving him a shove, and he fell over backward. Hard.

For a few moments, I stood there, trembling and gasping, half expecting him to get up and grab me again. But he didn't move.

The sound of Lucie's voice behind me made me jump.

"Is he dead?"

CHAPTER 16

I pushed him on the shoulder with my foot. Nothing. His head seemed to be in deep shadow, twisted as it was to one side. Tentatively I bent down to take a better look, then rolled his head over with my hand in order to better see his face.

My hand came away sticky. What I'd mistaken for a dark shadow was actually blood.

"I think I've killed him!"

I turned to look at Lucie as an icy terror gripped my insides.

"What am I going to do?" My voice was starting to rise hysterically, and I felt like I couldn't catch my breath. "I didn't mean to kill him...I just wanted him off me..."

"We have to *go!*" said Lucie. "Before anyone sees us. *Come on!*"

I stared at her for a moment, then realized she was right. We had to go.

We wheeled our bicycles onto the road, and I stood there dumbly for a moment, unable to remember the way home.

"This way!" Lucie called.

I followed her blindly, completely unaware of where we were, certain that any second, I'd be surrounded by soldiers pointing their guns at me. In my mind, I went over and over what had happened. *He attacked me. He was trying to rape me. I was only defending myself.* Which would count for nothing, I knew. Any assault on a German soldier was punishable by death, regardless of the circumstances. *But would they know it was me?*

I came to a screeching halt as it hit me.

"Lucie, stop!"

She turned to look back at me in frustration.

"The bottle! The champagne bottle! I have to go back and get it!"

"Oh, my god!" she wailed.

"It'll have my fingerprints on it!"

Back we went. My eyes were blurred with tears, convinced as I was that the alley would be surrounded by soldiers and guard dogs. *Or what if he's not there anymore? What if he was just unconscious? What if he got up and walked away? What if, at this very moment, he's reporting you to the authorities?*

As the nightclub came into view, we both dismounted.

"Stay here with my bike," I said to Lucie. I'll run over there on my own and get the bottle.

I could hear myself whimper as I ran along the side of the buildings and told myself sharply to be quiet. When I reached the alleyway, all I could hear was the music from the club. He was still there, lying in exactly the same position. The bottle was close to his body, probably covered in his blood, an incriminating piece of evidence that would easily have sentenced me to death.

But was he really dead?

I bent down over him for the second time. Took his wrist to see if I could hear a pulse, but I wasn't sure if I was doing it the right way. His eyes were closed, which meant he might just be unconscious. No, I couldn't take any chance of him still being alive. Taking the bottle, I positioned myself over his upturned head, closed my eyes, took a deep breath, and smashed it down with every ounce of strength I had left.

Gripping the bottle in hands that were slick with sweat or blood—I didn't know which—I staggered back toward Lucie as the bile rose into my throat and retched into the gutter.

I was trembling from head to foot as we made our way home in the pre-dawn light, arriving utterly spent, sick at heart, and more afraid than I'd ever been before in my entire life.

⚜

Once we got home, we were both too exhausted to talk. I lay in bed with my head throbbing from where my hair had been pulled, eventually dozing off to gruesome visions of my brother Jacques lying on the ground as I hit him on the head with a bottle. I awoke to the sound of my own screams, feeling sick, dizzy, and disoriented, straining my ears for the sound of jackboots marching up the stairs and hammering on the door.

When I was sure that Marie had left for work, I got up and made a cup of the bitter-tasting chicory coffee we were forced to drink and sat at the kitchen table until Lucie joined me.

"I can't face going to work today," she said, sitting down heavily and rubbing at her bloodshot eyes.

"You have to go!" I said. "We have to act as normally as possible!"

Neither of us spoke for a minute.

"Do you think they've found him yet?" she whispered.

"Of course they have!" I snapped. Her face fell. "Sorry, I didn't mean to yell. I just keep thinking of all the witnesses in there that saw me dancing with him. And then, how many people saw him follow us out of the club?"

"Most of them were too drunk to remember anything," Lucie pointed out. "And anyway, who would suspect girls like us of…"

"Murder?" I finished her sentence for her. *And such a vicious murder, too. Smashed on the head and again on the face. Who could commit such a brutal crime?*

The sound of a truck close by on the street drew me to the window. But there was nothing there.

"We have to act normal," I said to Lucie again. "Should we go and do the shopping together?"

She nodded in agreement. I was relieved—I didn't want to be on my own in case they came for me. *Not that Lucie's presence would stop them.*

All the while we were out shopping, my head kept spinning with random thoughts. The mere sight of German soldiers made me jumpy, and when I went to buy a newspaper from a boy on the street, my hands were shaking so much I could barely hold onto it. Lucie took it from me and scanned the front page.

"No, nothing there," she said.

It wasn't until later that Lucie dropped her bombshell. We were standing miserably in the queue for the bakery.

"At least I get to go to the movie theater on my day off," she said.

"What? What do you mean? Who are you going with?"

"That nice man I met last night. Kurt. We're meeting outside the theater at seven o'clock."

"Nice man you met last night? Have you lost your mind?"

The women in front of us turned around to look at me curiously, and I realized I had practically shouted.

"You can't go out with him. It's out of the question!" I said, turning away from the women ahead of us and lowering my voice.

"I don't see why not!" Lucie said, glowering at me.

"Lucie! You'll end up saying something to him! Or, he'll figure it out for himself."

"Of course I won't say anything! And how could he figure it out for himself? How could he know?" She turned away impatiently, and for a second, I thought she was going to leave.

"Lots of ways! Let's talk about it at home," I said through gritted teeth.

"Fine!" she said abruptly, with a frown. "Let's do that!"

As we inched our way closer to the bakery, neither of us spoke. We bought the bread, then went to the grocers for our three allotted eggs in complete silence. By the time we arrived back at the apartment, I was about ready to explode in anger. And so was Lucie.

"He'll figure it out!" I said as soon as I slammed the door shut behind me. "It'll be *all* over the newspapers, probably on billboards everywhere too, and he was *there!* He saw us leave, and he probably saw...*him*...leave, too!"

"That doesn't prove a damn thing!" said Lucie, banging the bread down on the counter.

"No, but the Germans won't see it that way. Don't you get it? They're going to do everything they can to find me so they can make an example of me!" I choked up and started to cry, feeling sick to my stomach. "And that means a firing squad!"

"If it's any consolation, we're both in this together," said Lucie. "It won't be just you in front of the firing squad. But I think you're exaggerating it out of all proportion. You said yourself we should behave like normal. So isn't he more likely to ask questions if I *don't* show up at the theater?"

We argued off and on for the best part of an hour. All I was asking was for her not to go out with him. Why couldn't she accept that? Eventually, I felt too tired to continue. She had made up her mind she was meeting him, and nothing I could say would change her mind.

Maybe she'll reconsider, I thought, as I left the apartment to go and see my brother.

Not looking forward to the long, dreary afternoon alone with Jacques, I pulled down "Winnie the Pooh," as I so often did. Usually, Jacques would have little or nothing to say. But today was different.

"No!" he said.

I sighed in frustration. "But you like Winnie the Pooh. It's what Papa used to read to us!"

"I know," he said. "But I'm too old for that now."

"Oh!" I said, taken by surprise. "I suppose you are too old for it, now that I think about it!"

As Jacques browsed through the books on the shelf, I spoke without thinking. "Do you remember him? Papa? Do you remember what he looked like?"

For a few moments, he didn't speak, and I thought I'd lost him. But then he stepped over to the mantle and took down a framed photograph. I'd forgotten it was there—our parents on their wedding day.

"You look just like him, you know," I said, fighting back my tears.

"I know," came the abrupt reply. He replaced the photo, went back over to look through the books with his back to me, and I knew the conversation was over.

A long afternoon was followed by a long evening behind the bar. All I could think about was my impending arrest.

Now that the police had had the best part of a day to investigate the murder, they must have come up with some leads. Every time a German looked in my direction, I practically froze in fear, waiting for the accusatory point of a finger.

"*There she is! Arrest her!*"

But it didn't happen.

"What's going on?" asked Sacha when he first saw me that night. "You look like you haven't slept in a week!"

"Nothing!" I answered, shrugging him off as usual.

"Why don't I believe that?" he said. "I've never known anyone gets in so much trouble as you, Lulu. Only thing is, I never get to hear all the juicy details because you never tell me anything!"

"I promise to tell you *everything* when this goddamn war is over!" I replied.

⚡

News of the murder hit the headlines the following day. Lucie and I were barely on speaking terms, and I had gone out on my own specifically to buy a newspaper. When I looked at the front page, I felt my knees start to buckle and was afraid I might faint. Breathing heavily, I made my way down the street back to the apartment.

"Oh, no," said Lucie as soon as she saw the paper.

German Officer Murdered Outside Paris Nightclub

Paris police report that yesterday morning, on February 25, 1941, the body of a German army officer, Leutnant Heinrich Schmidt, was found in an alleyway next to Le Caveau nightclub in the 8th Arrondissement of Paris.

According to the police report, Leutnant Schmidt had suffered at least two blows to the head with a blunt object.

"We have not as yet identified the weapon," says a police spokesperson. "We are in the process of following a number of leads.

We urge anyone who was in attendance at Le Caveau on the evening of February twenty-fourth to contact us."

General von Rauschenbaum, the German army commander of Paris, says he will stop at nothing to find the culprit behind this heinous crime.

"I view this act as a direct attack on the German Reich. The perpetrator should turn himself in before I consider putting reprisals into effect."

"Why are they saying two blows to the head—you only hit him once. And what does he mean by reprisals?" asked Lucie.

"I don't know. Lucie, *please, please* don't go out with that fellow. I think it's a really bad idea."

She sighed. "All right, *all right!* I give in! You win. I won't go out with him if you feel that strongly about it."

"Thank you," I said with relief.

But she'd turned her back on me and didn't respond.

CHAPTER 17

There was a rift between Lucie and I that didn't seem to want to go away. She was resentful of me for preventing her from seeing the man she'd met, and I was dumbfounded that she would put our lives in jeopardy for the sake of a date with a German. We no longer did the morning shopping together, and the idea of going out together after work was unthinkable—not just because of the memory of that night, but also because we didn't want to be seen out together, in case it jogged anyone's memory.

The following day's headlines said that a manhunt had been launched for the killer.

Killer.

That word had never entered my head until that moment. I was a *killer? Don't think that way,* I told myself. *You were defending yourself. You didn't mean to kill him.* Then I focused on the word "manhunt," which was good because it suggested the "killer" was a man.

Constantly looking over my shoulder, and flinching in anticipation at the sound of footsteps outside the apartment door, the next few days dragged by with agonizing slowness. Four days after the event, I was so worn out from worrying that I briefly considered turning myself in—a thought that left my head almost as soon as it entered. I wasn't brave enough to face a firing squad.

Starting my shift one evening almost a week later, I was beginning to feel a tiny tinge of hope. The police must have interviewed everyone they could at this point, I reasoned. And the more time passed, the better my chances of being overlooked.

"Lulu, you have to take a bottle of brandy and two glasses up to room 304," said Sacha.

"What? No, I'm not a waitress. Why are you asking me?"

"I'm not the one doing the asking," said Sacha. "*You've* been requested!"

I felt the blood drain from my face. "By whom?"

"Captain Hartmann, apparently. Don't know why he wants you, but there you go."

Hartmann? Oh, no! That's the creepy old General's name. But he's a general, not a captain. Sacha must have got it wrong.

Why he wanted to see me could only be one of two things. Either he's figured out I was the one who abandoned him on New Year's Eve, or…he's going to arrest me for murder. It was like walking to my own execution, foolishly carrying a tray with brandy and two glasses so that my captors could toast my demise.

I took the hotel elevator for the first time, whisked upward while serenaded by soft, soothing orchestral sounds. Stepping out at the third floor, I marveled at the lushly carpeted hallway and the cheerful glow of the rose-colored wall lamps. *Luxury, indeed,* I thought. Such a waste on these crass German officers.

"Enter!" called a voice when I knocked.

I carried the tray over to the desk, noting with relief that the man sitting behind it wasn't the General after all. This man was much younger. But why had he asked for me in particular? Bracing myself for the worst, I stared at the floor in front of me and waited for him to speak.

"You don't remember me, do you, Louise?" he asked in German.

I looked at his face and saw that he was laughing. *That face. Yes. The blond hair, strong jawbone, and crinkly blue eyes.*

"It's me, Hans! We met in Munich in thirty-seven!"

"Of course I remember you!" It had been four years. He had filled out a little, I noticed but was just as striking as ever. Perhaps even more so.

"We spent just a few hours together, but you always stayed in my mind," he said, moving away from his desk. "Come, sit with me for a few minutes!" He pointed to a sofa and coffee table on the other side of the room."

"But I'm supposed to be working!" I don't know if I was smiling more because of him or because I was still a free woman.

"No buts!" he said. "I'm the one giving the orders around here!"

An odd tingle went down my spine. That was exactly what the General had said to me in the nightclub on New Year's Eve.

I sank into the plush velvet sofa, admiring the huge vases of fresh flowers placed strategically around the room, the heavy brocade curtains, and the delicately patterned wallpaper, as Hans poured me a brandy.

"Prost!" he said as we clinked glasses in a toast. "I only arrived in Paris yesterday to start my new position here. And as soon as I walked into the bar last night, I recognized you! I can hardly believe my good fortune!"

He put his glass down on the table, then looked at me earnestly.

"I'm sorry. I don't mean to pry. But, are you married?"

"No!" I laughed.

"Betrothed, perhaps?"

"No—there's no man in my life!" That wasn't quite true. I still longed for Taddy. "But tell me all about yourself. You're a captain now?"

"Yes, I've done well. I was sent to Czechoslovakia, then Poland, and now here I am in Paris. With you."

Enveloped in that steady blue gaze, my heart flipped, just as it had four years ago. I was that impressionable seventeen-year-old girl again, enthralled, enamored, and infatuated. But it couldn't work. How could it possibly work out between us? And Sacha would be wondering what had happened to me.

"I really have to get back to work," I said, standing up to leave.

"Can we talk more later?" he asked. "When do you finish work? Perhaps you could join me for a late supper."

"I should be free by midnight," I said. I wasn't at all sure I was doing the right thing by agreeing to meet him, and I knew that Sacha, for one, would disapprove if he found out.

But we're just old friends, after all. It'll be fun to talk to him. What harm can there be?

When I got back to the bar, Sacha gave a sigh of relief.

"Thank goodness you're back," he said. "What took you so long?"

I knew Captain Hartmann from when I was in Munich in 1937, I tried to explain. He's just an old friend, and we were just catching up. Really.

Sacha rolled his eyes at me and shook his head. Predictably. And when Hans came down to the bar at half past eleven to wait for me, Sacha pulled me aside.

"Is that him? Your so-called old friend?"

"Yes," I said irritably. "That's him. So what?"

"He just arrived at the hotel yesterday. Do you know what he *does*?

"No, but I'm sure you're going to tell me."

"Counterintelligence," said Sacha with a knowing look. "So you'd better be *very* careful!"

I didn't know what counterintelligence was—probably something to do with the Germans spying on the French in search of trouble-makers--but I wasn't about to say as much to Sacha. I felt his eyes boring disapprovingly into my back as I left the bar with Hans. Once we arrived at his room, any doubts evaporated when I saw the amount of food and wine set out on the table. Fresh crusty bread, cold chicken, an array of cheeses, olives, and fruit. I had never felt so hungry.

"What have you been up to these last few years, Louise?" he asked as we ate and drank.

Oh, not much. Working for the Resistance. Getting into trouble with German generals. Murdering the odd soldier here and there. That sort of thing. Oh, and I was going out with a German Jew for a while. But I don't suppose that's something you'd want to hear about.

"Trying to stay out of trouble, mainly," I said.

"Ah, yes, I can believe that. I remember how you insisted on paddling in the stream in the park in Munich. You even took your stockings off, as I recall!"

Happy, carefree times. What wouldn't I give to go back to that moment.

The meal over, we stood side by side at the balcony window to look at the view. The city was in darkness because of the blackout, but I could make out the Eiffel Tower in the distance when the moon peeked out from behind the clouds.

"This is my first time here," said Hans. "I will be in need of a guide. Would you volunteer for such an arduous task?"

How could I resist? He was standing so close to me that I could smell his masculine fragrance and feel the heat from his body. His skin was healthily smooth and tanned; his body strong and taut. Ignoring an urge to fall helplessly into his arms, I moved away and sat back down on the sofa.

"Of course! Where would you like to go?"

We talked for a while about what Paris had to offer, then I forced myself to get up and leave. He showed concern when he learned that I was cycling home and wanted to send me in a car, which I adamantly refused. I also adamantly refused his offer to walk me outside the hotel to my bicycle—it really wouldn't *do* to be seen walking out of a hotel with a Nazi officer.

On the way home, I wondered what on earth I was getting myself into.

He's a Nazi, a Jew-hating Nazi. You know that because you remember very well what he said in Munich. What would Joséphine think of you for stooping so low? And think about Taddy. You're betraying your friends.

Yes, I berated myself. But, as usual, I also made excuses for myself.

I'm not hurting anyone if I see him from time to time. After all, he's just an old friend. He's not my enemy—I'm not even French. It's not my war. And anyway, he's the most handsome and charming man I've ever met. Why can't I have a little bit of fun in my life for once?

Having convinced myself that I would be doing no harm by accompanying Hans on his sightseeing tours, I decided it would be wise to keep it to myself. No one needed to know— not Sacha, not my mother, and not even Lucie. But it didn't work out like that. The following evening when I had just started my shift behind the bar, Lucie came in. She stood at the far end of the bar and gestured impatiently for me to come over.

"What the hell are you doing? You tell *me* that I can't see *my* German soldier, and yet you're off seeing a Captain. In his room, no less! That's why you were late home last night! And you were deliberately hiding it from me! You're *despicable!*"

"No...you don't understand..." I began. "How did you find out?"

"How did I find out? It really wasn't that hard, Louise. I think everyone who works here knows about it by now."

"But, he's just an old friend..."

"I bet. And you're not *my* friend anymore! You just can't be trusted."

I was left feeling stunned. She'd got it all wrong. And when I tried to explain it to her later, she not only refused to listen, she said perhaps I should pack my bags and leave the apartment. I was furious that she could be so stubborn and did as she suggested.

The following morning, I got up early and moved out without even saying goodbye.

Upon finding out that I had moved back in, my mother was unsympathetic.

"You know you always have a home here, Louise," she said with a sigh. I sighed, too. Being back home with my mother was the last place I wanted to be.

CHAPTER 18

I found out from Sacha that my shifts had been changed. On Fridays and Saturdays, I was to work only from one to eight o'clock, and I was to have every Sunday off. Sacha was vexed because it left him short-staffed at the busiest times. I realized that Hans must have requested these changes without conferring with me first and felt slightly put out. For a while, anyway.

The next time I saw him, he was standing at the bar with the very man I'd been trying to avoid for several weeks—the General. I desperately tried to look as if I was busy elsewhere, but eventually, Hans called me over by name, so I had no choice but to go over and greet him.

"Louise, I'd like you to meet my uncle, General Hartmann."

Uncle! That explains why they both have the same name.

The General bowed graciously as if he'd never met me before.

"Louise is an old friend of mine, Uncle. We met in Munich a few years back."

The General's eyes never left my face. "Is that so?" he asked.

Replaying in my head the horrifying moment when he was breathing wetly into the side of my neck, I shuddered inwardly, smiled brightly, and busied myself in getting them another drink.

"Dinner on Friday, Louise," said Hans. "Meet me in the lobby at eight-thirty. My driver will be waiting."

Hastily glancing around to see if anyone had overheard, I couldn't help but feel put out. His invitation had felt like an order; I would have preferred to have been asked rather than told. *Still, I'm not about to quibble when there's dinner involved, am I?*

※

On Friday after my shift, not having much choice with regard to what to wear, I changed into the black silk dress I had worn on New Year's Eve, presuming we would be going somewhere sophisticated. On my way to the lobby, I couldn't help but peek cautiously into the dining room as I passed, praying that Lucie wouldn't see me all dressed up. She'd know who I was going out with, and she wouldn't be pleased. Luckily for me, I didn't see her and hurried past the open restaurant door like a criminal.

Hans was standing near the door, looking at his watch, as I approached. He was wearing what must have been a dress uniform—a light, dove-gray tunic with a high, stand-up collar, silver buttons down the front, and a silver belt. With ribbons and braiding across his chest, braided breeches, and high black boots, he stood straight and tall, the embodiment of Nazi power and supremacy.

My face flushed as he looked me up and down in appreciation.

"You're on time. Excellent! And you look beautiful," he said, guiding me through the door with his hand on my back. "Here is the car."

The uniformed driver opened the door for me as I slid into the back seat, inhaling the unmistakable scent of leather.

"Maxim's," Hans commanded the driver as he seated himself beside me.

"Maxim's?" I asked in astonishment. The most famous restaurant in the world, not just in Paris, Maxim's was frequented by the famous and the wealthy. And apparently, these days, by high-ranking German officers.

"How did you manage to get a reservation there so fast?" I asked. "It's supposed to be almost impossible to get a table there."

"I made the reservation last week," he said. "I believe Hermann Göring has a table there tonight. We'll be in good company."

I didn't know who Hermann Göring was and didn't ask. I did wonder about his comment about making a reservation last week, however. He'd told me that he'd arrived on Tuesday—three days ago. *Never mind,* I decided, *it's nothing worth pursuing.* And I certainly forgot all about it when we entered the restaurant. The flickering glow of candlelight, red velvet chairs, a group of musicians playing softly in one corner—and most of all, the overwhelmingly delicious aroma of food. Most of the diners were German officers, interspersed with a few wealthy French couples, I noted; their eyes fixed on me speculatively as we were shown to our table.

"Mademoiselle, Monsieur," murmured the waiter as he expertly seated us. When the wine list and menus appeared as if by magic, I felt myself wanting to giggle at the formality of it all, but Hans looked so serious I didn't dare laugh. He studied the menu with a frown, and I glanced over its contents and almost shrieked in amazement.

"Ha! No food shortages here, I see!" I said without thinking. Hans smiled, then clicked his fingers at the waiter and proceeded to order for us both. I would have liked to have been consulted, of course, but wasn't about to object when I wasn't the one paying. My eyes were drawn to the table closest to us, where a rather portly gentleman was tucking into a shrimp cocktail. Then, when a basket of bread was placed on our table, it was all I could do not to rip into it.

Behave like a lady, Louise.

"This is wonderful," I said in appreciation to Hans. "Thank you for bringing me here!"

"My pleasure," he responded. "It's important to be seen in the right places. With the right people."

I wondered if by "right people," he was referring to me or to the high-ranking officers around us.

"May I ask exactly what it is you're *doing* in Paris, Hans?" I asked as the waiter poured Hans a mouthful of white wine to taste. "I know you're a captain, but what do you do?"

"Excellent!" Hans nodded his approval at the waiter, who poured a small amount into my glass.

"A toast, Louise. To us!" We clinked glasses, and he looked at me intensely. "As for what I'm doing in Paris, I'm following the Fuhrer's plan to create more living room for the Aryan people. As soon as all is in order, we will organize the settlement of a million German peasants into certain areas of France so that the French-speaking population will become completely Germanized."

"Oh." I honestly had no idea how to respond to that, fascinated as I was by the fervent expression in those blue eyes.

Caviar was placed on the table in front of us.

"Unfortunately, we are still dealing with the Jewish question." *How I would love to run my fingers through that hair. It shines like gold in the candlelight.* "The Jews, of course, are wholly responsible for the war, seeking the destruction of Germany with their lies and deceit."

Consommé, along with more wine. Absolute heaven.

"We are, of course, on track to eliminate them from civilized society. Along with the gypsies and the feeble-minded. Once we have dealt with the Jews' world conspiracy, we will be able to fulfill our destiny as the master race."

Steak with tiny new potatoes. The very smell made my mouth water.

Didn't Miriam use to make these for us? No, don't think about Miriam. Or Jacques.

Red wine to accompany the steak.

"But I am talking far too much! Tell me more about yourself and your family. Your mother teaches at the University, I believe?"

How did he know that?

"How did you know that?"

"Because you told me, of course!"

"Ah. My mother. She is perfection—in what she does and how she looks. Unfortunately for me, I can never measure up…"

On I talked, entertaining him and making him laugh, skipping over the existence of my brother. No funny stories to be had there. Another refill of the red and a chocolate tart appeared in front of me, probably the most divine thing I had ever tasted in my entire life. Hans nodded and smiled at all the right times and, at one point, reached for my hand across the table. His touch sent an electric current through my body.

"You're very beautiful, you know," he said. I blushed.

Cheese, foie gras, crackers. Brandy.

"Now *I'm* talking too much," I said. "Tell me about your family!"

He told me he was from Nuremberg, an only child born into a military family. "It was expected that I should join the Hitler Youth Organization to continue the family tradition. My father distinguished himself in the Great War, you see. He died of a heart attack last year."

Pulling a photograph out of his wallet, Hans showed me a family portrait—his father, in full military uniform, standing stiffly behind his wife; she sitting on a chair, staring unsmilingly at the camera in a long, dark-colored dress with a high neckline. And there was a young Hans perched on one knee in front of his mother, an intense frown marring his fine features.

"My father was a great man. Herr Hitler himself spoke well of him." Putting the photo back into his wallet, Hans paused. "He was strict, demanding...sometimes he and I didn't see eye to eye. But he was only doing his duty as a father; I understand that now. One day perhaps, you will come to Nuremberg to meet my mother."

I would travel the world for you. Especially if I get to eat like this all the time.

To my astonishment, Hans stood up, bowed, and offered me his arm. "Shall we dance?" he asked. On the small dance floor, he pulled me close, and I felt the tantalizing warmth of his hand through the thin fabric of my dress. I laid my head on his chest and, to the tune of "Parlez-Moi D'Amour," fell unequivocally, unconditionally, head-over-heels in love.

When we left the restaurant that evening, Hans gave the driver my mother's address. *How do you know where I live?* I wondered. But I didn't ask him that, of course, basking as I was in the afterglow of the most romantic night of my life.

The car pulled up outside, and I hoped no one was watching. Especially my mother.

Opening the door on his side, he walked around to help me out. A chaste kiss on the cheek left me longing for more, and I opened the gate to let myself in as he stood watching. As I closed the gate behind me, I heard the car pull away and stood still for a moment of self-doubt.

You know you shouldn't be doing this…

Which quickly evaporated.

A person can't help who she falls for. What does it matter that he's the enemy? Makes no difference to me, and it's not like I'm hurting anyone.

When I went inside to a mercifully dark house, I realized that I hadn't brought any food home for Jacques.

Next time, I promised myself.

CHAPTER 19

The following day being a Saturday, Maman was home. She wasted no time in giving me a shopping list and sending me out into the cold to queue up for hours on end. Thankful that she hadn't seen me arriving home the night before in a fancy car, I did as she asked without complaint. Keeping my relationship with Hans a secret was going to prove difficult, I realized, especially if he insisted on driving me home every time we went out. But for now, I didn't want her or anyone else to find out. She'd only get angry.

I returned home with our measly rations later that morning to find Claude sitting at the kitchen table with Maman. My heart sank as I anticipated what he was about to ask me.

"Hello, Louise," he said, standing up from the table to face me. "I'm here to ask for your help again. For tonight. Look, I realize you don't want to get further involved with us, and I wouldn't ask you if I wasn't desperate. This will be the last time, I promise."

I squirmed inwardly. If Hans ever found out that I'd been helping the Resistance, he'd see it as the worst type of betrayal. To my mind, my relationship with him was more than casual. Hadn't he mentioned me going to Nuremberg to meet his mother? And didn't that show that he was serious about me? Perhaps the thought of us getting married had already crossed his mind. From my perspective, he was smart, handsome, and ambitious—perfect husband material. And yes, he might be a little obsessive about certain things. Jews, for example. But that wasn't his fault. It was what he'd been brought up to believe. I was sure he'd change his mind or soften his stance about that, given time.

I thought I might have a future with him, and I didn't want to jeopardize that. But I couldn't think of an excuse.

"I don't know. I'm really tired," I said. It sounded pathetic, even to me. "And I don't know how much help I would actually be. I get a bit panicky, you know…like when the dog barked at me that time…"

"Louise! Really!" said my mother in exasperation. "I can't believe you're being so selfish. These people are putting their lives at risk to help people escape. Have you *any* idea of all the work going on here? All Claude is asking you to do is keep watch for a few minutes!"

Claude raised his hand as if to say, enough. "It's quite all right, I understand."

But my mother wouldn't give up. She placed her hands on her hips, pursed her red lips, and frowned at me.

"I just *don't* understand you sometimes, Louise!"

"All right, all right!" I snapped. "I'll do it!" Standing outside in the dark and cold, waiting to be stopped and interrogated by a Nazi patrol, seemed infinitely more preferable to being verbally attacked by my mother. I knew if I didn't agree, she'd never let me forget it.

I was to show up at a certain abandoned warehouse at midnight, Claude explained. I should stand outside the gate and keep an eye out for patrols. If I saw one, I should signal a warning with my flashlight, walk toward the Germans, and show my credentials if asked.

"Warehouse? Why a warehouse?" I asked.

"It's where they're hiding people," said Maman. "Foreign Jews. Sometimes British airmen. From there, they'll be smuggled onto a barge and out of the city."

"Let's not say more than we have to, shall we, Margarite?" said Claude. "No need for her to know the details."

"Sorry, Claude," said my mother, putting her hand over her mouth apologetically.

Not for the first time, I gave some thought to the operation I was helping. Smuggling food was one thing. But people? Claude was evidently part of a much larger organization. Suddenly, I thought about Taddy. Such a pity that he couldn't have had help to escape before the Nazis took him.

I quickly brushed away thoughts of Taddy; there was no point in thinking about him anymore. But that night, as I waited outside the gates of the abandoned warehouse as instructed, I strained my eyes to catch a glimpse of the escapees. From what I could see, there were three of them, being stealthily escorted, one at a time, from the building to a waiting truck. One of the figures was so small and slight that I thought it must be a girl or perhaps even a child.

If they were inside the truck as yet, I didn't know, but then headlights and the sound of an engine were heading straight toward me. I heard myself groan and quickly pointed my flashlight toward the warehouse door, turning it on and off as instructed. Then I mounted my bike and pedaled toward the oncoming vehicle. Caught in its headlights, I froze as a voice shouted at me to halt.

I waited and waited, stamping my feet to try and keep them warm and rehearsing in my head what I should say.

Hello, officer. What am I doing out here this time of night? None of your business. Go away and bother someone else.

Good evening, officer. What am I doing out here this time of night? You may well ask. Helping a few unfortunate souls escape from Nazi brutality, actually.

Officer—it just so happens I am very good friends with Captain Hartmann. He won't be too pleased with you for questioning me, by the way.

Finally, a uniformed figure approached, demanding to see my papers. As he came closer, the light of his flashlight shining directly on my face, I did my best to smile and look friendly.

"Of course, officer. Here you are," I said in German, holding out my documents. "I work nights at the Lutetia Hotel. That's why I'm out so late. Umm, you look familiar. Have I perhaps served you at the bar?"

On and on, I babbled—something I know how to do well—as the soldier glanced at my papers.

"It all looks to be in order, Mademoiselle," he said with a smile. "I haven't been to the Lutetia, but maybe I should?"

"Oh, yes. It's such a popular place for officers such as yourself. There's also a restaurant, and the food is supposed to be magnificent..." I talked for so long that finally, another soldier jumped out of the truck and called over.

"What's going on?"

"Nothing, nothing," replied my new friend. "I'm coming!"

I even waved them off before turning back to the warehouse and flashing an all-clear signal. A minute later, the truck carrying the escapees rolled away in the darkness, and I headed for home feeling immensely proud of myself for saving the day.

My efforts didn't go unnoticed.

"Claude says to pass on his thanks for what you did the other night," my mother said to me a couple of days later. "You saved those people's lives, you know."

I shrugged.

"He also says if you ever change your mind about joining them…"

I shook my head. "No, it's not for me. Thanks anyway."

Definitely not for me, especially now that Hans is in my life.

∗

Hans got into the habit of sitting at the bar for a few minutes while I was working. Not that he would be drinking— sometimes he would ask for a glass of water, saying he always liked to keep a "clear head." Despite the sour looks from Sacha, I was always elated to see him and often found myself looking toward the door in the hope of seeing him.

He always seemed concerned for my well-being.

"It's raining out," he said one day. "Would you not prefer my driver to take you home tonight so you don't get wet?"

I turned him down, but his thoughtfulness prompted me to consider asking him for extra rations at home. That would mean telling him about Jacques, however, and I wasn't sure I was ready for that as yet. *I'll wait until I've known him a little longer,* I decided. *Then I'll ask.*

Toward the end of that week, I had just started my shift when two policemen in blue uniforms entered the bar. They went over to Mitzi, who was wiping off one of the tables and spoke to her. I couldn't hear their words but knew exactly what they were asking. As she turned and pointed in my direction, my scalp prickled, my brain told me to run, and my body remained frozen in fear.

They know. They've found out I killed the German soldier.

They've come to arrest me.

CHAPTER 20

"Louise Bellingham?"

I nodded furiously, having lost the ability to speak.

"Police," said the officer, holding up his badge. "We'd like you to accompany us to the station to answer some questions."

Best to try and sound innocent, I decided. *Outraged; upset; confused, perhaps? Or should I act more unconcerned?*

"Questions? What questions? Am I under arrest?" I knew I sounded slightly hysterical, and tried my best to calm down.

"No, Mademoiselle. We're not arresting you. You'll find out what it's about at the station."

I turned to give Sacha a look, but his face was unreadable. He said nothing, not a single word of encouragement. Feeling as if the entire hotel—guests and staff—were staring, I walked out of the bar toward the lobby between the two policemen. We passed by the restaurant, and I wondered if Lucie had been taken in as well. Then I realized in horror that we had never discussed what we would tell the police if we were ever asked about that night at Le Caveau. Should I tell them that

I was there, or should I say I've *never* been there? What would Lucie have said?

A blue police van was parked outside, the back door was opened, and one of the men helped me up the step and inside. Sitting on a hard bench, I held my nose at the stink of sweat and vomit, then flinched when the door slammed shut, leaving me in the dark.

No wonder it smells so bad in here, I thought, as the van lurched and bumped its way along the streets of Paris. By the time it came to a stop, I felt dizzy and nauseous, still unsure of what I should say about the night of the murder.

"Paris Police Prefecture," read the plaque on the building. I was escorted straight through the reception area to a room devoid of any furniture except for a table with benches and told to wait. It was agonizing. *Why didn't we have the sense to come up with a story?* I kept asking myself. Then another thought occurred to me. *What if Lucie has told them everything? She probably hates me enough to do that. What if they know everything, even about the murder weapon? Oh, good lord, what did I do with the bottle? I don't even remember...*

I started as the door abruptly opened, and a man with a Hitler-like mustache entered.

"Good day, Mademoiselle. Detective Choux."

Choux, meaning "cabbage." I hid my smile, which soon disappeared off my face as he started his questions. What was my full name, where did I live, who else lived in my household, how old was I, where did I work?

As I answered, he quickly wrote down my answers in a notebook. The questions kept coming fast, barely giving me time to think.

How long had I been working at the Lutetia Hotel? What was my mother's full name? When had I last been out of the country? What hours did I work at the hotel? Who were my friends?

Who were my friends? I hesitated. *Better not mention Lucie. But should I tell him about Hans? I couldn't decide.*

Mr. Cabbage stared at me intensely for a moment, scribbled something, then fired his next question.

"Where were you on the night of Saturday, February twenty-fourth?"

Oh my God. He knows.

"Umm, February twenty-fourth?" I stalled. "I would have been at work. I work late, you see."

The cabbage leaned closer. "And do you not sometimes go out after work?"

"Umm, sometimes, I suppose. But not at all often!"

"Did you go out after work on February twenty-fourth, Mademoiselle? It's just over two weeks ago. And a Saturday. Surely you must remember something so recent?"

"I would, but there's nothing to remember. I'm sure I just went home after work as usual."

"Have you ever been to Le Caveau?"

I struggled to stay calm as he watched my reaction.

"Le Caveau? You mean the nightclub?" I asked as calmly as I could. "I think so, but I'm not sure how long ago." I changed my tone, wanting to sound annoyed. "Look, can you just tell me what all this is about? I'd really like to get back to work!"

I took a breath, intent on making my displeasure known, when there was a knock, and the door opened.

"Inspector Choux, may I speak with you for a moment?" said a uniformed policeman.

The cabbage left; the door closed behind him. My heart was pounding, my palms slick with sweat. *I just have to keep on denying everything*, I thought, fighting back the urge to moan and cry. *But what if they take me to the SS?* Sacha had told me rumors about the SS headquarters on Avenue Foch, where suspects were interrogated and tortured. *Maybe it would just be best to confess and be executed…*

The door opened, and Cabbage entered, holding the door open.

Oh, no, this is it! I'm being transported out!

"Wait!" I said, about to blurt out my confession.

"Mademoiselle, you are free to leave," he said, gesturing for me to exit the room.

Free to leave? I didn't understand until I walked through the door into the reception area and saw a familiar tall figure in full Nazi uniform. Exuding an unmistakable air of power and authority, he cast a cold stare at the cabbage.

"I expect to hear no more of this matter, Detective. Do I make myself clear?"

The cabbage bowed his head in acquiescence, then met my eyes as he pursed his lips. He knew I was guilty. But Hans didn't.

"Heil Hitler!" Hans saluted the detective, who gave him a half-hearted arm raise in return, then turned to me. "My car is outside."

My hero. He had saved my life. I trembled as I realized how close I'd come to death.

"Louise, you're white as a sheet," he said once we were settled into the back seat. "We'll go back to the hotel and get you some brandy. I find it hard to believe the utter incompetence of the Paris Police. Suspecting *you* of having something to do with a *murder?*"

I shuddered.

"Totally incompetent! I have no patience for such imbeciles!"

Back at the hotel, Hans took me to his room, where I sat on the sofa as he wrapped a blanket around me and took me in his arms. "One would only have to look at you to know that you're incapable of such a crime! My poor darling!" He kissed me gently. "I've sent down for that brandy. It should be here momentarily."

And it was. Brought in by Mitzi, who almost dropped her tray when she saw me sitting there. She looked away from me immediately as if we'd never met and backed out of the room hurriedly. But my embarrassment didn't end there. Hans had also ordered dinner. Although I had never actually engaged in conversation with the waiter who brought the food, I could tell that he recognized me by an imperceptible raise of his eyebrows.

It's none of their business, I told myself. *They have no right to judge me. This man saved my life. And I love him.*

Much to my relief, Hans started talking about other things and didn't mention the police incident again. But I couldn't put it behind me. The look on Detective Cabbage's face kept haunting me. He almost had me, and he knew it. I really didn't know if I was free and clear or not.

Hans, being so caring, wanted his driver to take me home, but I insisted on riding my bicycle, telling him the fresh air would do me good. On my way out of the hotel, I went into the restaurant and quickly spotted Lucie. She frowned when she saw me.

"What do you want? I have nothing to say to you!"

"Lucie! I was taken to the police station today! They were asking me about…what happened."

Her face drained, and she held on to the nearest chair for support. "Oh, lord. What did you tell them?"

"Nothing! I said I wasn't there. And I didn't mention you!"

She looked at me with hate in her eyes. "*You're* the one that got us into that mess, so you'd better *not* mention my name!"

Honestly, you call yourself a friend? Now leave me alone and go back to your Boche boyfriend!"

She walked off, leaving me stunned. That was so unfair. I was doing her a favor by warning her, and all she did was throw it back in my face. If she were a real friend, she'd be concerned for me, and she'd be happy for me for having found Hans.

Everyone was being so judgemental!

CHAPTER 21

On Sunday, I was to meet Hans for a day of sightseeing. Where we were going, he wouldn't tell me.

"It will be a lovely surprise," he said,

We arranged to meet at the hotel at eleven o'clock on Sunday, which suited me fine because I didn't want him pulling up outside the house in full daylight. Just as I was about to leave, however, Jacques noticed that I was going somewhere and wanted me to take him to the park to sail his boat.

"I can't take you now, Jacques. I have to go out!"

"No-o-o!" cried Jacques, sitting on the floor with his head in his hands. "I want to go to the lake!"

"I'll take you tomorrow, I promise," I said, patting him on the head. But he wouldn't have it; he held onto my hand and cried. He was so thin these days—as were we all—but Jacques looked like he was starving…gaunt, with dark circles under his eyes. I felt guilty for leaving him, but couldn't keep Hans waiting.

"Tomorrow, I promise," I said again, pulling myself free of his grasp.

"Where are you going?" asked Maman, entering the room to see what all the fuss was about.

"Just out with a friend," I said and left the house quickly before she could ask any more questions.

I realized by the expression on Hans' face that I must have been late. He was standing outside the hotel and looked at his watch and frowned when he saw me.

"Hans!" I said. "Have you been waiting long?"

"A few minutes," he said. I could tell he was irritated by the way he was tapping his foot, but he kissed me on the cheek and led me to his car.

"Where are we off to?" I asked.

"The most famous landmark in Paris!" he declared. "The Eiffel Tower!"

"Oh, no," I said. "I'm sorry, but we can't. It's closed to visitors right now!"

Joséphine had told me the story several months ago. When it was learned that the Germans were going to occupy Paris, a group of resisters cut the cables to the elevators. As a result, when the Nazis had wanted to fly their swastika from the top, the soldiers carrying the flag were forced to take the stairs all the way to the top—a total of 1,665 steps. One small victory for the French, as Joséphine had gleefully explained it.

"Not today," said Hans. "Today is a special opening, especially for German officers. Only as far as the first floor, I'm afraid. It seems the elevators are not functioning."

I wondered if he knew why they weren't working but wasn't about to ask. On this bright, sunny day, I didn't see any need to upset him. I was determined to have a good time. Sinking back into the luxurious leather, I smiled as Hans held my hand and informed me there was to be lunch served at the tower.

Today, I wouldn't want to be anyone else but me, I thought smugly.

People are always in awe of the enormity of the Eiffel Tower when they see it up close for the first time, and Hans was no exception. As we walked toward the entrance, we tilted our heads back to look upward.

"It was built in 1887 for the World Fair by Gustave Eiffel," I informed Hans. "And at first, there were a great many protests because people thought it was so ugly."

"It's true that construction began in 1887," said Hans. "But the first floor was achieved in 1888 and the very top not until 1889."

"Oh," I said, feeling foolish.

"It took two years, two months, and five days to construct." Hans smiled in satisfaction. "Also, I believe it consists of 18,038 metal parts."

"Oh."

"And once it was finished, it received two million visitors at the World Fair, and the criticisms ceased."

So much for my efforts as a tour guide.

We made our way up the steps to the first floor. Three hundred twenty-seven steps, to be precise, according to Hans, who led the way. Trailing along after him, I admired how effortlessly he climbed, strong, straight-backed, and vigorous, never feeling the need to hold on to the handrail. Every now and then, he would stop, turn around, and politely ask me if I needed to rest.

"No, I'm fine," I lied every time. I had the feeling that for him, it would be a sign of weakness to falter. At the halfway mark, my legs started to burn, and I was breathing heavily, but I wasn't about to tell him that.

The stairway was wide, providing plenty of room to overtake other groups of mainly older German officers. Every time we did so, Hans offered an "excuse me, please," and of course, the inevitable "Heil Hitler!" When we finally reached the first floor, my legs felt as if they were about to give way, while Hans gave the impression that he could run down and back up again with no problem.

"Excellent!" he said, offering me his arm. We strolled around the observation deck, taking in the spectacular view and marveling at how tiny people looked from such a vast height. Then we entered the restaurant and were seated at a table complete with a white tablecloth, silverware, even a vase of fresh flowers. A thought occurred to me.

"Oh, my goodness. They would have had to carry all this upstairs since the elevators aren't working!"

"Indeed!" Hans laughed, obviously unconcerned by the amount of effort that must have gone into the preparation of the event..

It was a cold luncheon comprised of chicken, ham, quiche Lorraine, bread, salads, and champagne. I wondered if I'd be able to put some of the food in my bag without Hans noticing. Then I wondered if he was aware of the food shortages that the rest of us were forced to endure.

"You know," I said carefully, "the French don't have access to good food anymore because of the rationing."

"Yes, I am aware of that," he replied. "I myself went without luxury foods and alcohol for years when I was a part of Hitler Youth. Those things can do harm to your body. I am always careful not to over-indulge, and I keep myself healthy through athletic activity and systematic physical exercises."

"You do look very...healthy," I said, glancing appreciatively at his magnificent physique. "But it's not just luxury foods they're being denied. A lot of people are going hungry." I bit my lip, wondering if I'd overstepped.

"I suspect the French aren't used to any form of self-discipline," he said with a smile. "It will do them no harm to limit their food intake for a while. Self-indulgence is what made the French so inefficient. But enough about them! Tell me what you've been doing since I saw you last. Other than your terrible experience of the other day, that is."

Yesterday I had to line up for half an hour to get turnips and carrots, then again for the three eggs we're allowed, along with a pathetic-looking piece of fish that we would only have given to the cat before the war. Other than that, I argued with my mother and upset my brother. Oh, I also helped the Resistance transport some people—probably Jews—out of Paris. Just normal, everyday things.

I racked my brain for something interesting to tell him, then remembered the letter.

"I received a letter from my old friend Emma in London." The letter had taken five weeks to arrive. Opened and re-sealed, parts of it had been heavily crossed out in black ink. "Emma was with me the day we met for the first time. Do you remember?"

"How could I forget?" he asked, leaning across the table to take my hand.

"Emma's coming to Paris to stay with her aunt. She's ill and needs looking after."

"I'll look forward to meeting her again," said Hans. "And what of your mother? Is she well?"

"Yes, she's well."

"Excellent! Is it just the two of you living there?"

I hesitated. *Should I tell him about Jacques? Why was I reluctant to do so?* But the decision was taken out of my hands. Mercifully, another officer approached our table, greeting

Hans effusively. It would appear they had served together in Poland. The man asked Hans what he was doing in Paris—the exact same question I had asked a while ago, only to have received a garbled response about eliminating the Jews.

"Counterintelligence," replied Hans. "Specifically, the investigation of acts of sabotage against the Reich."

My hands prickled with sweat as I felt my face flush. *He couldn't possibly know, could he? Of course not. No need to worry,* I told myself. *In any case, my Resistance days are over.*

Lunch over, we returned to the observation deck to look across the river. His arm around my waist, I pointed out various landmarks, and he told me that the following weekend he would be taking me to the Moulin Rouge.

"I feel on top of the world! Here in Paris. With you," said Hans, gazing at me with those intoxicating eyes of his. "But come, it's time for us to descend."

Feeling a little tiddly after all the champagne, I leaned into him as he practically carried me down the steps with his arm firmly around me. I sighed happily as we stepped outside, having reached solid ground. But Hans stopped abruptly and frowned.

"Where is the car? I don't see the car!"

"Wait here!" he commanded and walked off, looking in every direction for the missing vehicle, constantly checking his watch.

"This is unacceptable!" he said, coming back to join me. But just then, the car arrived and pulled up in front of us. The driver got out and walked around to open the back door.

"How *dare* you!" Hans shouted at the man. "How dare you leave your post? This goes against all the rules! You know you should wait for me at all times!"

"I'm sorry, Captain," said the driver. A fair-haired boy probably not yet twenty years old, he had turned bright red and looked distinctly intimidated. "I thought I'd have time to fill the car with gas."

"*No, no, no!* This was not the time for errands! Due to your stupidity, we had to wait here with no idea as to when you might return!"

Feeling uncomfortable and more than a little embarrassed, I spoke up.

"Hans, it's all right, really. No harm…"

"Louise, I'd thank you to keep out of this. This man is my responsibility!" He sighed. "We shall speak about this later. In the meantime, do your job and *drive!*"

Hans gave the driver my address. I didn't want to be dropped off outside my house but figured it wasn't a good time to argue. *Hans has every right to be strict with his driver,* I told myself. *After all, he's an officer in the army. Discipline is important.*

As we rode, he took my hand in both of his and told me what a memorable day he'd had.

"Me too, Hans," I replied. "Thank you for taking me. It was unforgettable."

When we pulled up outside the house, I saw my mother watching through the window. And I knew the day was about to become even more unforgettable.

CHAPTER 22

I was confronted by my mother as soon as I closed the front door behind me.

"So!" she practically spat at me. "Would you care to explain?"

"Explain what, exactly?"

She folded her arms and tapped her foot impatiently on the floor. "You know very well what!" She jerked her chin toward the door. "Him! The friend you went to meet today! A *Boche*?"

"Yes, he's German. So are you! So what?"

"*So what?*" She was raising her voice now. "So what, you ask? I'll tell you what! He's the *enemy*, that's what! He's a Nazi! I may be German, but I am no Nazi! That man wants to exterminate anyone who's a Jew—do you remember our friends Miriam and Joséphine? —and *because* of him, we're all practically starving to death!"

"You don't understand..."

"What is there not to understand, Louise? You're going out with a *Nazi*! Don't you understand how foolish that is, not to mention dangerous? Just the other day, you were helping the Resistance. What if your Nazi *friend* finds out about that?"

"He won't! I'm not as stupid as you think I am. I *know* him! I met him years ago in Munich. And I like him. He treats me well!" I almost added he saved my life but didn't want to go into an explanation about that.

"I'll bet he does." Standing in front of me, she took me by the shoulders as if she wanted to shake me, looked into my face, and lowered her voice threateningly. "Break it off with him. Before anyone gets hurt."

A surge of anger rushed through me. "No, I won't. I've had enough of you telling me how to live my life!"

I tried to walk away, but she grabbed me by the arm. "Louise, it's not just about you, don't you see that? You're putting all of us at risk!"

"That's ridiculous," I said, shaking her away from me and heading for the stairs. *Why did my mother always have to be so critical? And so dramatic? It's not as if the war will last forever.*

Hans and I are like Shakespeare's Romeo and Juliet, I decided. But in our case, there could only be a happy ending.

⟶

The following week, as we were having dinner together at La Petite Chaise with a glorious view of the river, Hans asked me if I'd be interested in a different job.

"You're wasting your talents in the bar. With your ability to speak French, German, and English, you'd be an asset to our unit. As a civilian, of course."

He clicked his fingers for the waiter to come over. "Another bottle!" he commanded. I wondered idly how many glasses I'd drunk.

"We are in need of someone to do some translations and answer the telephone on the third floor," Hans continued. "You'd be like a receptionist, but you'd be translating letters and documents as well."

It sounded quite boring to me. Also, I liked my job behind the bar. Although Sacha and Mitzi weren't too friendly toward me anymore.

"It would be a day job, from nine to six, very easy to do. You'd get weekends off, too." He leaned forward and took my hand. "We'd be able to spend more time together!"

"That sounds nice," I said uncertainly. "Do you mind if I think about it?"

"Not at all!" said Hans. "Tomorrow, I'll show you where you'd be working. That might help convince you!"

I imagined that it would mean working in luxurious surroundings, and I was right. The following day, Hans arrived at the bar and insisted I take a break to go up to the third floor.

"I'll be back in ten minutes," I said to Sacha. He shrugged and turned away hurtfully. Nowadays, he would only speak to me if it was absolutely necessary. *Perhaps I should consider the new job,* I thought. *After all, it's not too pleasant working with people who seem to hate you.*

"COUNTERINTELLIGENCE" read the sign in bold lettering outside the door. The suite of rooms had been converted into offices. Sunlight danced on an enormous polished desk as I breathed in the gratifying scent of leather from the sofa and chairs, and my feet sank into the depths of a lush carpet. I felt the warmth of the spring air from the open balcony door and couldn't help but smile in appreciation at the vases of golden daffodils placed all over the room. Hans opened the door to an adjoining room where a woman sat at a typewriter.

At least I wouldn't be asked to do any typing, I thought, remembering my miserable failure as a would-be typist at the secretarial school I'd attended.

"This would be your workstation," said Hans, turning back to the large desk in the daffodil-filled room. "I think you'd find it quite pleasant."

"May I ask…I mean, I'm not sure…what *is* counterintelligence?"

He hesitated before answering. "For the most part, we investigate acts of sabotage against the German army. And we do our part in the elimination of the Jews. But all you have to do is look pretty—as you always do—perhaps translate some documents occasionally and direct callers or visitors to the right person."

It all sounded so deceptively innocuous, so matter-of-fact. But from these luxurious surroundings, the Germans were hunting down resisters like Claude, Joséphine, and André.

And myself.

No, I'm not a part of that anymore, I told myself.

You're no longer a part of the Resistance. Fine. But by working here, doesn't that put you on the side of the Nazis?

No! All I'd be doing is answering the telephone! I'm still neutral.

The door opened, interrupting me from my thoughts. It was the General. He looked at me for a moment before speaking to Hans.

"There you are, my boy. May I have a word with you? In private?"

"Excuse me," said Hans, following his uncle out of the room. The door wasn't closed all the way, and after stepping a little closer, I could make out what they were saying.

"She speaks German and French fluently; English too, Uncle. She's perfect for the job."

"All you want is to get her into your bed. And don't tell me otherwise," growled the General. "Are you sure we can trust her? Have you done a background check?"

"I have, Uncle," said Hans. "She is who she says she is. And anyway, I've met her before, so I know her. She has no sympathies toward the French, I promise you."

"Very well. But I'll be doing my own investigation. There's something about the name that's bothering me. Bellingham."

"Very well, Uncle. Heil Hitler!"

"Heil Hitler!"

"So, what do you think?" Hans asked as he escorted me back down to the bar.

"It's beautiful! But I need a little time to think about it," I said, looking up at him and wondering about that background check he'd mentioned.

"Of course! I know you'll make the right decision, Louise!"

As I worked at the bar for the rest of my shift, I thought it through. Taking the job would alienate everyone I knew, but that didn't matter so much because they all appeared to hate me anyway. Hans would be pleased, and I'd get to spend more time with him.

He was the most important person in my life, after all.

\\//

The following morning, I was sitting on the sofa watching Jacques play with his train set. I had practically decided to take the office job, which would mean I wouldn't be home to look after him during the day. Maman would have to rely on Miriam to take over. I anticipated my mother's reaction when I told her about the new job. She'd be infuriated for a number of reasons. *But how was it fair*, I asked myself, *that she could work during the day and expect me to stay home? And how dare she judge me for my career choices? Why, this job could lead to all sorts of important opportunities. The war isn't going to end any day soon, so we might as well all get used to that.*

I'd worked myself up pretty well when the doorbell rang. And there, standing at the door with a big smile on her face, was Emma.

We hugged each other tightly.

"I've missed you so much!" I said.

"Me, too," she said. It's so good to be back in Paris. We're being blown to bits in London. You wouldn't even recognize the place."

Emma described her journey across the Channel and told me about her aunt, who was hardly able to look after herself anymore. The teachers' college she was studying at had been hit hard by German bombs and forced to close, she said.

"So here I am—to look after my aunt and spend time with my dearest friend! Now, tell me all your news!"

I made coffee, and we sat at the kitchen table. It was just like old times.

"I've met someone!" I said to her. "And I really, really like him!"

"Oh, Lulu, I'm so happy for you," said Emma, squeezing my hand. "Who is he?"

"As a matter of fact, you've met him!"

As I jogged her memory and reminded her of our time together in Munich, her smile started to fade. And when I told her that Hans was now a captain in the German army and was working in counterintelligence, she started to look anxious.

"You're going out with a German officer? A Nazi?"

"No, not just any old German officer. It's Hans! Do you remember how gorgeous he was? Well, he's even more handsome now, if that's possible!"

"Lulu! He's the *enemy!*"

I stood up from the table and held my head in my hands. "Why does everyone keep saying that? He's not! He's just doing his job. It's not his fault he was born German."

"Oh! So, he's working *against* Hitler, is he? Trying to stop the bombs, standing up for the Jews, sabotaging those godforsaken concentration camps…?

"No! Of course not! You don't understand!"

"Obviously, I don't," said Emma.

I turned away from her to lean against the stove, and neither of us spoke for a minute.

"Look, Lulu," said Emma as she rose from the table. "I don't want to fall out with you. You're my best friend. But please, I beg you, reconsider!"

I went over to her and hugged her. "All right," I said. "But come over to the bar one night this week before curfew, and I'll buy you a drink!"

"Sounds like fun. I'll do that! I've never been to the Lutetia before."

We parted on amicable terms, but I had no plans to reconsider my relationship with Hans. Emma would come around to my way of thinking, I decided. Especially if she got to meet him again and saw how charming he was.

CHAPTER 23

Fast asleep in bed after a long shift at the bar, I awoke in fright when I felt someone shaking me.

"Louise!" It was Maman bending over me. "I need you to come downstairs. Now!"

Groggy and perhaps a little hungover—I'd had a couple of brandies with Hans in his room after work—I fumbled for my robe and went downstairs, wondering what on earth could be wrong.

"In here," whispered my mother from the kitchen.

The light wasn't turned on; only a single candle sputtered on the kitchen table. I shivered in the gloom, then noticed a figure seated at the table.

Claude.

Why are you here at this time of night? I was about to ask. *And if you want my help again, the answer is no.*

"Sorry to wake you," he said. "But I have to be careful. Just as a precaution, you should both be aware that you might be being followed."

Did he wake me up to tell me that?

Both Claude and my mother were looking at me intently. "Claude has some news," said Maman. "About the warehouse."

I realized she must be talking about the abandoned warehouse where they were hiding people, but didn't see how that could be any of my concern.

"What about it?" I asked, wishing Claude would just leave me in peace.

"It was raided today," he said. "By the Boche."

"That's a shame," I said, doing my best to sound concerned. *Why is he telling me? There's nothing I can do about it.*

"We believe that somebody must have tipped them off."

A silence as they both watched my face. I was outraged.

"What? *You think it was me?* You think I would tell the Germans about the warehouse?"

"Calm down," said Claude tersely. "You're *seeing* a Nazi officer, are you not? He's counterintelligence, from what I understand. So does that not make you our primary suspect?"

I leaned back in my chair and gasped.

"What have you been telling this fellow?" he asked.

"Nothing, nothing! You're crazy if you think I would betray you! I would never tell him anything!" My mind was racing, trying to remember exactly what I had said to Hans. "And anyway, wasn't I there to help on two occasions? So I'm just as guilty as anyone else involved!"

His expression, in the flickering light of the candle, was unmoved. Accusing.

"I'm not sure you understand the repercussions this could cause," he said, lowering his voice. "Two people were taken. Do you know where they were taken to?"

I shook my head.

"Well, then, let me enlighten you. They would have been taken to Nazi Counterintelligence Headquarters. Avenue Foch. Do you know what goes on there?"

I shuddered and nodded in answer to his question.

"Torture. They will torture those poor souls for as long as they can keep them alive until they get some information out of them. They *will* talk, you know. We're all at risk."

My mother put her head down on her hands and groaned.

"Listen, I promise you I've never said a word…" I said.

Claude stood up to leave. "Very well," he said. "But you might give some thought as to whose side you're on."

With that, he headed to the front door, as my mother followed him to see him off, and I escaped up to my room and curled up in bed as the tears started to flow. *How could they even think that I would do such a thing? Even my own mother! After I put myself out to help them, too! Well, they can accuse me all they like, but I'm not giving up Hans just because they say so. He's the love of my life. We're destined to be together…*

I cried myself to sleep.

∿

The following day as I left for work, I noticed a black car parked up the street and could see that someone was sitting inside. Was someone watching me? After overhearing what the General had said about conducting an investigation into me and with what Claude had said about being followed, I suddenly felt vulnerable. Pedaling toward the hotel, I stopped several times to look behind me, but the black car was nowhere to be seen.

All in your head, Louise, I said to myself. *Stop tormenting yourself.*

Not long into my shift, I was happy to see Emma arrive at the bar. I made her sit at the far end, so we could chat out of earshot of Sacha and offered to make her a cocktail.

"Do you remember when we drank champagne at school?" I asked. "We wanted to learn how to be sophisticated, so we practiced drinking and smoking."

"I do remember that." Emma smiled. "You were a wild one. Still are, for that matter. But no, I don't want anything alcoholic." She looked nervously around the room. "I don't know how you can stand working here, to be honest."

I looked around, unsure of what she was referring to. The bar looked as it always did—elegant, clean, and comfortable. A couple of tables were occupied by officers, but they were speaking quietly amongst themselves.

"Them!" she said in a whisper, tilting her head toward the men. "Nazis!" And she visibly shuddered.

"Oh, Emma, they're not monsters, you know." I stopped, suddenly visualizing the beatings I'd seen on the streets. "Well, not all of them, anyway."

I poured her tomato juice and asked about her aunt.

"She's a lot better now that I'm here to look after her. At least now she has me to shop and cook for her."

My heart leaped as I saw Hans walking toward us. What perfect timing! Now Emma could talk to him. She'd be sure to understand why I'd fallen for him once she'd gotten to know him.

"Hello, Louise. This must be Emma! Hans Hartmann, at your service! I believe we have already met."

He held out his hand courteously to Emma, but she didn't take his in return. Instead, she turned away and picked up her handbag as if to leave.

"Sorry, Lulu," she said. "I can't go along with this."

Mortified, I reached across the counter to take her arm but, in the process, knocked over the glass of tomato juice. The red liquid spread across the counter and then started to drip onto the floor. Seeing Emma halfway across the room, I ran around the bar and caught up with her just as she was entering the lobby.

"Emma!"

She turned to face me. "Lulu, you shouldn't be seeing him. It's wrong."

"How can it be wrong?" I asked. "You haven't even given him a chance!"

"Look," she said, "this isn't 1937 anymore. There's a war on. And that man—the man you think you're in love with—has a lot to answer for. If he's wearing that uniform, that means he's evil, Lulu. Evil. Just like his precious Fuhrer!"

I stepped away from her in outrage. *How dare she call Hans evil?* She didn't even take the time to speak to him. Poor Hans, his feelings must have been hurt by her disgraceful behavior. Hurrying back to the bar, I apologized to him as best I could.

"She's just upset because her aunt is so ill. It has nothing to do with you!"

"Don't worry," he said with a smile. "Will you come up for a nightcap when you're done here?"

I nodded in relief and set to cleaning up the spilled juice, which was starting to congeal on the floor.

Like spilled blood.

\|/

Tired of everyone turning against me, I informed Hans that I'd be glad to take on the receptionist job. When I told Sacha that I was leaving the bar to work on the third floor, I didn't get the reaction I'd anticipated. He looked worried.

"Lulu, I know we don't see eye-to-eye, but are you sure about this?"

"Quite sure, thank you," I said snippily. "I know what I'm doing!"

"Actually, I don't think you really do," he said. "He's using you, you know."

Using me? What does he mean?

"I'm not doing anything wrong by working for the Nazis. Plenty of people are doing the same thing, including the Paris Police, in case you hadn't noticed."

I felt tired of defending myself all the time. They should all mind their own business. I was old enough to make my own decisions. And as for Hans "using me," that was preposterous.

My first day—the following Monday—I arrived at my new office promptly at nine o'clock, and finding it empty, waltzed around the room admiring the pictures and the view from the window before sitting down at my desk, upon which sat a shiny, brand-new telephone. I had only used a telephone a handful of times in my life and felt somewhat intimidated. And next to it was a strange-looking box with a row of buttons.

"Fraulein Bellingham!" A young German entered the office and introduced himself as the telephone technician. "I'm here to show you how to use the new equipment. It's quite remarkable, let me tell you!"

Within twenty minutes, I'd been taught how to take an incoming call and put the caller on "hold" if needed. The box turned out to be an intercom, with which I could speak to people in the other offices along the hall without leaving my desk. All so modern and sophisticated. I pivoted around in my chair a few times, waiting for the phone to ring, then became aware of the sound of the typewriter in the adjoining room. Deciding I should introduce myself, I entered the room.

"Good day," I said. It was the same older lady I'd seen there before, tapping away at the machine. "I'm Louise. I'm starting work here today."

Barely raising her head, the woman gave me a cursory glance, a quick nod, and continued to bang away at the keys.

"I tried to learn how to type once," I said. "It really is quite hard."

Sighing almost imperceptibly, she paused her typing and looked at me pitifully. "Ingrid," she said abruptly. "Now, if you don't mind…"

I took the hint and escaped back to my own room. A search through the desk drawers revealed pens, pencils, and paper, after which I found nothing better to do than to gaze out of the window for what seemed like forever. Eventually, an officer I recognized from the bar came in with a pile of letters.

"You're the translator, right? Here—these letters need to be translated into German, please. All we need is a rough transcript of what the person is asking. It doesn't have to be word for word."

I was intrigued. The letters were mostly handwritten, and all of them were in French. *Something to do, anyway,* I thought, *and it might even be interesting.* I picked out a letter at random.

To the Kommandant,

My neighbor is a Jew. His name is Josef Poirier, and he lives at 95 Rue Aubergine.

You should send your soldiers to take him away.

The letter wasn't signed.

"Unbelievable!" I said out loud. What sort of person would give up their own neighbor? I pulled out another letter.

Attention Abwehr.

The people in Apartment 201 at 56 Rue Marchand are going around defacing your posters. They are also very loud and rude people and should be arrested.

I almost jumped out of my seat as the telephone rang. Nervously, I picked up the receiver and said the line that I'd rehearsed.

"Abwehr. How may I help you?"

There was a brief silence before the caller spoke. It was a woman's voice. "I want to know how much you will pay me for information."

"What sort of information, Madame?" I asked.

"I'm not telling you until you tell me how much you pay!"

"You would have to come in and talk to one of the officers," I said. I had no idea if the Germans would pay for information or not, but that seemed like a reasonable response. The woman didn't seem too happy and simply hung up.

I continued working my way through the letters, attaching a brief translation as I went, and became increasingly appalled at how many people were selling out their friends, neighbors, and even family members. At the stroke of noon, Hans appeared at the door and, after a kiss on the cheek, informed me it was time for lunch.

"I always go to the hotel restaurant," he said. "It's so convenient."

It was the last place I wanted to eat. What if Lucie was working? Even worse, what if she waited on our table? She'd probably spit in my food.

"I'm not very hungry..."

"Nonsense! Of course, you are! Come along!" said Hans, looking at his watch and tapping his foot.

Reluctantly, I followed him to the elevator and down to the restaurant, where we sat at a large table already occupied by a handful of officers. I let out a sigh of relief when I saw that Lucie wasn't on duty, still feeling hugely self-conscious as I tried not to look the waiter in the eye. Hans asked me what I would like but then went ahead and ordered grilled lamb chops for both of us. Not what I would have chosen, but I knew he was just being kind.

"Tell me all about your first morning," he said.

I told him about the telephone call and the letters I'd been translating.

"You'll see a lot more of those," said Hans. "In the beginning, we ourselves were quite shocked at how easily the French turn on each other. But it makes our jobs a lot easier!"

"But do you pay people to give information?" I asked.

"No! Most of them only want to get revenge for their own personal reasons. But that's the French for you. It's no wonder they gave up so easily. No backbone. No sense of duty or loyalty."

Afterward, on our way back to the elevator, I thought for a moment that I glimpsed a familiar figure walking through the lobby.

"Maman!" I called, but she quickly disappeared through the door. I wasn't entirely sure it had been her. After all, I *had* drunk two glasses of wine over lunch.

CHAPTER 24

I knew I was drinking too much, but believed it was justified under the circumstances. And anyway, shouldn't I be allowed to have a bit of fun in my life for once, I reasoned. I would have wine with lunch, an aperitif before dinner, wine with dinner, often followed by cognac afterward as a "nightcap." Hans and I went out for dinner a few times a week, frequenting all the best restaurants in Paris. My favorite spot was the Moulin Rouge, which had been turned into a dance hall because of the war. There, with Hans' strong arms around me, we would sway to the music of a young singer by the name of Edith Piaf, whose songs always tugged at my heartstrings.

Sometimes I would go back to his hotel room afterward. With his arm around me, we would sip cognac and listen to music on his gramophone—Mozart being his favorite. When the kissing became too intense for my liking, I would gently push him away. It's not that I didn't like it—I did, too much so—but I didn't want to end up sleeping with him.

"I'm not that sort of a girl," I said to him on one occasion. He apologized, told me he understood, and I knew I'd said the right thing. The thought of marriage was already on my mind; I wanted him to respect me.

If I felt any guilt about leaving Maman and Jacques to fend for themselves, I reminded myself that they could at least share my rations. And I was taking extra food home.

Hans had come into the office with a frown.

"Why didn't you tell me you had a brother?" he asked.

My heart skipped a beat. Why hadn't I? *You know very well why you haven't,* said a malicious little voice in my head. *Because Jacques is considered feeble-minded. He's expendable, along with the gypsies and the Jews.*

"Oh!" I said brightly. "I suppose it never came up!"

Hans looked at me intently. "I would like to meet him," he said. "And your mother, too, for that matter. How about if I take you all out to dinner?"

My heart sank. I couldn't think of a way out of this one. "Well, I'll ask her. She's very busy at the University, though, so I don't know when it would be."

"Ah. Does your mother not approve of our relationship?" he asked with a forced smile.

"Of course she does," I lied.

"Well, then. Please convey my regards, and let her know that I am eager to make her acquaintance."

"Yes, of course. Thank you," I said. He was so thoughtful, but there was no way I was going to pass on his message. I couldn't think of a worse nightmare than having my mother even meet him, let alone sit down to dinner with him.

But from that point on, Hans started giving me gifts to take home. Chocolate bars, a bag of fresh oranges, an expensive bottle of wine for Maman. One day, a box of luxury food items was delivered to the door. I was afraid that Maman would refuse to eat any of it on principle, but she surprised me by making no comment at all.

"By the way, was that you at the hotel the other day around lunchtime?" I asked her. "I thought I saw you."

She turned away from me so suddenly that I knew it must have been her.

"No, of course not! Why on earth would I need to go to the Lutetia?"

Why indeed? I wondered. We didn't spend that much time together, but I noticed that she seemed low-spirited of late. I sometimes caught her sitting alone, smoking and staring into space, suddenly busying herself with her newspaper articles when she realized I was looking at her.

"Are you all right?" I asked.

"Yes, yes," she said, rubbing her eyes. "I'm sorry. Sorry."

I'd never heard my mother apologize for anything before. "Sorry for what?" I asked. But she wouldn't answer. Just shook her head and left the room.

⋇

The cherry trees were blossoming; vendors were selling tulips, lilies, and daffodils on every street corner, the sun was warming the streets of Paris, and I was hopelessly in love. I worshipped everything about him: the way his eyes crinkled up at the corners when he looked at me, his smooth tanned skin and perfect white teeth, the confident and decisive way he addressed his soldiers. On the battlefield, I decided, he would be an intrepid warrior, a fearless leader, a conquering hero.

Yes, sometimes he could be impatient and demanding, but that was because he expected others to strive for the same level of perfection as himself. How happy I would be to share my life with him, to stand dutifully at his side as he climbed the ranks of the German army to become a superior officer.

Perhaps we could live in Munich, in a beautiful cottage on the outskirts of the city with a view of the mountains. We would have two golden-haired children, a girl, and a boy...

"Louise!"

I blinked to see Joséphine standing before me in the sitting room. "Sorry, I didn't hear you come in!"

"Did you hear the news?" she asked, frowning at me in a way that suggested I'd done something wrong.

I shook my head in annoyance. There was always news. How could I be expected to know what she was talking about?

"I should have thought you would have since you work for them," said Joséphine, placing her hands on her hips defiantly.

That was unkind. I said nothing and waited for her to explain.

"A German naval officer was shot and killed in the metro the other day by a member of the Resistance," she continued.

"Yes, I heard about that," I said, wishing she'd go away. I had no interest in talking about things like that.

"The Boche have killed three innocent French people in retaliation," she went on, her voice rising in distress. "Three! None of them connected to the killing, and one of them a woman!"

"That's terrible," I said.

"Oh, but you don't know just *how* terrible. There's more. Now they've put out an announcement to say that from now on, for every German killed, they will execute at least *ten* innocent French people."

As I fumbled for the right words, Joséphine stared at me as if I had made the announcement myself. I couldn't think straight for the thought that they might execute innocent people for the murder I myself had committed.

"Does that include murders that have already taken place?" I asked, suddenly finding it hard to breathe.

"No. I don't know," said Joséphine. "Maybe you should ask your boss."

With that, she sat down straight-backed at the piano, and within moments, her fingers were flying across the keyboard as she pounded out Chopin's Revolutionary Etude—written, as I recalled, in 1831 after Poland had been crushed after a failed rebellion against the Russian Empire. So heartrending was the music that tears filled my eyes. *Joséphine,* I thought, *you have so much to offer the world. Why don't you save yourself? A girl like you isn't going to win against the might of the German army.*

The news about the Nazis killing innocent people in retaliation bothered me. How were those people chosen? Was it completely at random, like drawing a name out of a hat? What if I were to be picked? Or worse, what if it was Jacques? The following morning at work, I voiced my concern to Hans, and he laughed.

"My darling Louise! Do you think I would ever allow anything to happen to you? Of course not! No, it's actually a convenient way for us to dispose of Jews, Communists, and other degenerates. Mostly those who are already in our custody."

I didn't know whether to feel relieved or not.

He straightened out the pencils on my desk. "How much do you know about Sacha, the bartender here at the hotel?"

His question took me completely by surprise. My first thought was of the secret slot under the bar, and, under his intense scrutiny, I scrambled for something to say.

"Sacha? Well, I worked with him behind the bar, as you know. But I didn't get to know him that well. Why do you ask?"

"Oh, his name came up. Nothing to concern you, really." Hans turned to the balcony window. "Listen, it's a beautiful day. I'm taking a drive out to the countryside—there's some business I want to attend to. Would you care to accompany me? We could have lunch out."

Sounded like a dream come true to me. I rested my head on the soft leather backrest as we sailed smoothly along winding country lanes surrounded by lush green fields dotted with colorful wildflowers. You would hardly know there was a war going on. It all seemed so peaceful.

"What kind of business is it? Or shouldn't I ask?" I inquired, reaching over for his hand.

"A military operation is taking place in one of the villages. It will be over by the time we get there, but I just want to see for myself if all has gone according to plan."

I couldn't grasp what a military operation in a village might entail but was distracted by the sight of a farmer tending his crops, followed by that of a magnificent chateau perched on top of a hill. *Perhaps Hans and I should settle down in France,* I thought. *We could live in one of these quaint villages. I would bake my own bread and buy fresh eggs and cheese from a local farmer...*

The sweet fragrance of freshly mown grass was suddenly overpowered by the stench of smoke.

"What in God's name? Pull over!" Hans commanded.

As the car screeched to a halt, Hans jumped out and ran toward the smoke, taking his pistol out of its holster as he went. The driver followed likewise, and I was left peering through the windshield, alarmed by the sound of frantic screams and shouts from up ahead. Then, three gunshots in quick succession.

My heart was pounding, and my hands slick with sweat as I scrambled to open the door. I had to see. If it was Hans lying there dead or wounded, I didn't know what I would do. Through gaps in the smoke, I saw flames coming from a large wooden barn-like structure. A dozen or more German soldiers surrounded the building, their rifles pointed at a handful of civilians who were being herded toward an army truck. Jews, I guessed. This had probably been a hiding place for them as they tried to make their escape to the Free Zone.

Staying close to the car, I scanned the soldiers in an effort to find Hans. I had to know he was safe. And there he was, thank heavens, off to one side, looking every inch alert, attentive, and alive. My sigh of relief was interrupted by a sudden movement as a slight figure darted out of the barn toward the road. He had no chance, outnumbered and unarmed as he was, but nevertheless, he ran.

But as the figure approached, I saw that it wasn't a "he." It was a young woman of about my own age.

Within seconds, Hans had caught up to her, grabbing her roughly by the arm and forcing her to turn around. She looked up; for a split second, she and I exchanged glances, and I saw how alike we looked.

It was uncanny.

When Hans raised his gloved hand and hit her hard across the side of her face, I cringed in horror and clapped my hand over my mouth to stop myself from crying out. *Why did he do that? Why did he have to hit her? He shouldn't have done that.* Holding her arms cruelly behind her back, he pushed her over to the truck to join the other captives. When I saw him heading in my direction, I slid back into the car and took a few deep breaths to steady myself.

I didn't want him to know that I'd been watching.

"Sorry, darling," he said as I rolled down the window. "They made a right mess of things here. I just need to have a few sharp words with the Lieutenant, and we'll be on our way!"

I smiled at him weakly and watched as he strode over to the barn and shouted at some of the soldiers who were putting out the remains of the fire. There ensued an intense discussion with the Lieutenant, who kept shrugging his shoulders and pointing at the barn. Hans' "few sharp words" lasted a good ten minutes, during which I couldn't help but glance over at the truck, wondering about the fate of the poor brave girl who'd tried to escape. Finally, "Heil Hitlers" all around, and Hans was marching back to the car with a sour look on his face.

"His orders were simple enough!" he said once we were on our way. "I fail to understand why he thought it necessary to try and smoke them out. All his men had to do was break down the door, for God's sake. Starting a fire just made things messy."

He rubbed his eyes and rested his head.

"It's unnecessarily cruel, too, don't you think?" I ventured.

"Cruel?" He blinked in surprise. "Cruelty has nothing to do with it. These are Jews we're talking about. Inefficient, more like!"

The smell of smoke lingered in the car and on Hans' uniform for the rest of the day as a reminder of what I'd witnessed. Much as I wanted to know about the gunshots, I refrained from asking; I tried to push the entire episode out of my mind as we walked hand-in-hand along a pretty riverbank and enjoyed a delicious five-course luncheon at a charmingly picturesque inn.

It should have felt idyllic.

CHAPTER 25

Hans had taken me out for a glorious dinner at Maxim's. After several decadent courses that included escargots, coq au vin, and crème brûlée for dessert, I was satiated and slurring my words after long since losing track of how many glasses of wine I'd consumed. What we talked about during that meal, I have no recollection, but I do remember that I laughed a lot.

The memory of our trip into the countryside had been well and truly pushed aside. *I knew all along that Hans was a Jew-hater,* I reasoned. *So why should I be surprised by what he had done? When the war was over, that would all be behind us, and I wouldn't have to think about it anymore.*

After dinner, we took a romantic stroll along the River Seine. The warm breeze and the sound of the water lapping against the embankment suddenly reminded me of our time together in Munich. I was just about to drunkenly suggest that we take off our shoes and dip our feet in when Hans stopped walking and turned to face me.

He held onto my arms as I almost stumbled.

"I have something for you," he said, pulling a small velvet box out of his pocket. He opened it to reveal a gold chain with a heart-shaped locket. "This is to say that you have my heart, Louise. I love you."

It was what I had been waiting for all along—him declaring his love for me. I said all the right things, told him I loved him too; he placed the chain around my neck, we both admired it, kissed passionately, then, just for a moment, I wondered why my heart wasn't dancing with joy. *You've probably had too much to drink,* I told myself.

As was our habit, we went back to the hotel, where I sat in comfort on the sofa, and Hans poured us each a cognac. He pulled me in close, and exactly what we talked about, I'm not sure. The last thing I remember is Hans asking me about Joséphine. Even in my drunken stupor, I knew that I shouldn't be talking about her, but it was hard for me to focus on what I was saying. I was also seeing double.

When I awoke the next morning with a throbbing head and dry mouth, I was lying fully dressed on my own bed at home. Fingering the chain around my neck, I wondered how I had got there—the last thing I remembered was sitting on the sofa in Hans' room. *Had his driver brought me home? Had I come upstairs all by myself? Or...had someone helped me up here? Hans? Please, God, not my mother!*

By the time I got downstairs, Miriam had arrived to look after Jacques, and Maman was readying herself to leave. I wasn't about to ask her about last night in front of Miriam, and anyway, she seemed to be behaving as she normally did, without appearing to be more than usually angry with me.

Disturbed and unsettled about the whole blackout incident, I wished with all my heart that I had someone to talk to. Trouble was, I didn't have any friends left. Emma was annoyed with me, as was Sacha, and Lucie had made it quite clear that she hated me with a passion. I would go round to see Emma after work, I decided. Beg for her to give me another chance. After all, we'd been friends for so many years. How could she turn her back on me?

Quite easily, it seemed.

After a horrendously long morning of translating boring German documents into French with a splitting headache, I turned down Hans' request for me to join him for lunch. Actually, it wasn't a request at all, I realized. Hans always told me what I was to do and expected me to follow his directions. He was quite surprised when I insisted I did *not* want to go for lunch. The thought of greasy pork chops or chicken turned my stomach; plus, I couldn't help but feel annoyed at how fresh and rested he looked. Was it only me who drank too much? And what must he have thought of me?

I decided to find out.

"Umm, I think I might have had too much to drink last night," I said, too ashamed to admit I didn't even remember going home. Let alone upstairs to bed.

He laughed, showing those perfectly aligned, sparkling white teeth of his.

"Yes, you did. But no harm done. A good time was had by all!"

And that was it. No explanations, but no recriminations either. *Strange*, I thought when I was alone. *You would think that he, of all people, would object to excessive drinking. He always expects everyone to behave appropriately and follow the rules. Especially his rules. Unless…*another thought occurred to me… *unless he wanted me to get drunk so he could get information out of me.*

What was it Sacha had said to me? "He's using you."

Of course he's not using me, I told myself. *Ridiculous idea!*

Nonetheless, I went down to the bar with the intention of asking Sacha if he knew more than he was letting on until I realized he wouldn't be starting his shift for a few hours. Miserably, I went back to my office to answer calls from upstanding French citizens wanting to inform their neighbors while plowing my way through the translation of interminable German Foreign Office documents. As soon as six o'clock arrived, I hurried downstairs and cycled my way over to Emma's aunt's house.

I had so much to tell her. I wanted to show her the gold chain Hans had bought me and tell her that I thought he might soon propose. We could talk about the wedding. She would be my maid of honor, of course—how could she not be excited for me? I would ask her opinion—would it be best to wait until the war was over? Such a difficult decision that only a friend as close as Emma could help me with it.

Much to my relief, she answered the door when I rang. She eyed me suspiciously as she stood in the doorway with her arms folded in front of her.

"Emma!" I said. "Please, can we talk? I miss you so much! And I have so much to tell you! You won't believe what happened!"

"Are you still seeing...*that* man?" she asked with a grimace.

"Yes," I said, "but..."

"Well then, I don't know why you're here. I thought I made myself perfectly clear. I think you're wrong, so wrong, to be going out with *him*. A *Nazi*, no less. What are you thinking, Louise? Give your head a shake! Give him up!"

"But you don't even know him!"

"I wouldn't want to get to know him if he was the last man on earth. Open your eyes. Just look around you to see the atrocities they're responsible for. He's *one of them*, whether you like it or not. And I don't want anything to do with you anymore!"

She slammed the door shut, leaving me standing alone on the doorstep with tears in my eyes. How could she abandon me like that? Weren't friends supposed to be there for each other no matter what? Why was everyone being so morally righteous?

∿

Later that evening, as Maman, Jacques, and I were listening to the radio in the sitting room, we were surprised by a visit from Miriam. As she entered the room, Jacques ran over to give her a hug. She hugged him back without her usual cheerful chit-chat, then gazed despairingly around the room.

"Joséphine isn't here then?" she asked.

Maman and I looked at each other anxiously.

"No," said Maman. "I haven't seen her for a couple of days."

Miriam looked at me pleadingly, almost willing me to say that I'd seen her.

I shook my head. "Me neither."

Her face crumpled as tears filled her eyes. "She's gone missing. Since last night. They've taken her! I know they have! They've taken her!"

My mother had turned pale. "Now, now, Miriam," she said, "we don't know that for sure. She's probably visiting friends and forgot the time. I'm sure she'll be back soon."

Her words were unconvincing, and the expression on her face was one of fear. She led Miriam into the kitchen and busied herself making coffee as Miriam cried copiously into her handkerchief.

"I knew this would happen," she sobbed. "She puts herself at risk all the time with the things she does. It was only a matter of time before...before someone betrayed her."

Maman, standing at the kitchen counter with her back to us, froze with the coffee pot in midair. I knew what they were both thinking…that it was me who betrayed Joséphine. *And maybe it was me. Wasn't Hans asking questions about her last night? And wasn't I too drunk to remember what I told him?*

No! I would never betray Joséphine. No matter how drunk I was!

I felt enraged. Sick and tired of being accused all the time. I had done nothing wrong; why couldn't anyone understand that?

"You think it was me!" My voice came out louder than I had intended, but I didn't care. "Just admit it, both of you! You think I'm *conspiring* with the Nazis against all of you! You think that just because I'm going out with Hans that I'm a traitor! *Say it! Say it!* You think I informed on Joséphine!"

I was shrieking hysterically, but couldn't control myself. Jacques was cowering in the doorway, watching me with tears in his eyes, but I couldn't stop the venom.

"Why didn't you *leave* when you had the chance! Why in God's name are you still in Paris? You must know they're going to get you in the end. Not just Joséphine. All of you! You're Jewish! You don't stand a chance against them! When are you going to figure that out?"

The hurt in Miriam's eyes cut me to the core.

Maman turned around to face me, coffee pot still in hand. She was white as a sheet. "Louise…"

"Ha!" I scoffed. "Don't even speak to me, Maman. You've made it quite clear how you feel about Hans!" I was about to add that we loved each other and that she should get used to the idea of him as her son-in-law but suddenly felt spent, exhausted. I needed to leave.

"Louise!" called my mother, but I was already partway through the front door on my way to see Hans. I needed his reassurance. Pedaling my bike furiously along the road in the direction of the Lutetia, I tried to get my angry words out of my head, wishing I'd stayed calm. *I shouldn't have shouted at Miriam like that,* I thought. *That was cruel of me.* By the time I reached the hotel, I felt utterly miserable—angry, guilty, not to mention heavy-hearted at the thought of Joséphine being taken in for interrogation.

Hans would have to help, I thought. *What are you thinking? Hans isn't going to help a Jewish girl. You know that!*

On my way up to his room, I couldn't resist a peek in the bar. There was Sacha doing his favorite juggling trick with the lemons while Mitzi stood nearby, laughing with a man in an apron, who must have been the new bartender. *My replacement,* I thought glumly. How I envied them. How wonderful my life was when I had friends. People to laugh and have fun with.

Much to my relief, Hans opened his door to my knock and happily ushered me in. By the looks of things, he'd been sitting alone, listening to music and reading. The room looked cozy and inviting. Casually dressed in a short-sleeved shirt that showed off his muscular arms, Hans, too, looked inviting.

"Louise! Is something wrong? You look upset!"

I decided to get right to the point. "It's Joséphine. She's gone missing!"

He shrugged his shoulders, shook his head, and looked blank. "Who? Who's Joséphine?"

"You were talking about her last night!" I insisted. "The girl I know, the one who plays the piano—Joséphine. And now she's gone!"

Hans looked at me with amusement. "My dear Louise. I was talking about Joséphine Baker, the famous dancer, telling you that she used to stay here at the Lutetia! I certainly wasn't referring to your housekeeper's daughter!"

Housekeeper's daughter?

"How did you know she was my housekeeper's daughter?"

"Because you told me, you silly girl!" he said, kissing the top of my head. "But if this girl has gone missing, shouldn't someone contact the police?"

"Yes, of course," I said, feeling ridiculous for having come over here. What had I been expecting him to do? Confess that he'd been sounding me out for information about Joséphine so that he could have her arrested?

I felt utterly foolish. And confused.

"How about a nightcap?" he asked.

I wanted to leave. "Not for me—I think I had enough last night! I'll see you in the morning."

We kissed goodnight, and I left, anxious to apologize to Miriam for my heartless accusations. Arriving back home, I found Maman sitting alone, smoking in the kitchen. She looked up at me with a tear-stained face as I entered.

"Miriam left? I have to go find her and say I'm sorry," I said.

Maman nodded and cleared her throat. "You remember where she lives?" she asked tiredly.

"I do," I said abruptly. I didn't have the energy to get into a discussion or another argument with her and left without giving her the chance to say another word. Back into the night I went, thankful for the warm night air and the apparent lack of German patrols. Miriam's house was in the 11th Arrondissement, near the Place de la Bastille, little more than ten minutes from our house. The Bernhardts lived in a neighborhood alongside many other Jewish families. It wasn't until I had crossed the bridge over the river that I realized I'd left my bag at home with all my identification papers.

I stopped to think. *Damn! Should I go back or carry on?*

I was so close to Miriam's house that I decided to keep going. With no sign of any patrols so far, I figured I'd be lucky enough to make it. Even if I was stopped, I knew that nothing bad could happen to me because I was under Hans' protection. Even though, by rights, I shouldn't have a pass enabling me to be out after curfew because I was no longer working nights at the bar. But even if that came into question, Hans would smooth things over for me. He was like my guardian angel.

It must have been after ten o'clock—late to be dropping in unannounced—but I knew that the Bernhardts would still be up. Hoping that Joséphine herself would have re-appeared, I knocked at the door, and Miriam answered. Her tear-stained face fell when she saw me standing there, but it wasn't in her nature to be hostile.

"Miriam! I'm so sorry!" I blurted out. "I didn't mean any of those terrible things I said to you!"

She gave me a sad smile. "I know, I know you didn't, ma petite. Come in, won't you?"

I followed her through to the old-fashioned kitchen that hadn't changed a bit since I was a child. Her husband Aaron was at the table, looking a little grayer now, I noticed, his face lined with worry.

"Aaron went to make inquiries at the police station," said Miriam.

"Sit down, Louise, please," he said. "Yes, I filed a report, but they weren't particularly helpful. It's because we're second-class citizens now! I was born here in Paris, went to school here, worked all my life here. But suddenly, I'm worthless, treated like dirt, even when my beautiful daughter goes missing."

As tears ran down his face, Miriam patted him on the shoulder. "Let's not give up hope, mon chér. Louise, let me make you a cup of cocoa before you go. You must be tired!"

How she could be so affectionate toward me after all I'd said to her that night was a mystery. I'd known Miriam all my life and had always taken her endless kindnesses for granted,

I now realized. Even knowing that I was involved with a German officer, she was still sympathetic. I felt thoroughly ashamed of myself.

I sat for a while, talking about mundane things, while Miriam kept her gaze fixed on the door. At the slightest sound from outside, we stopped talking and strained to listen. Finally, I glanced at the kitchen clock to see that it was after eleven o'clock and decided I'd best leave.

Just as I was about to stand up, we looked at each other in alarm at what sounded like the arrival of a number of trucks or heavy vehicles. Men were shouting. *They're speaking French, not German*, I thought in relief. As Aaron went to the front door, Miriam and I stood behind him as he cautiously opened it to a blaze of light. Temporarily blinded, we shielded our eyes with our hands.

"Close it, Aaron, close it!" urged Miriam, and we stood uncertainly behind the door, listening to the uproar, not knowing what to expect.

We didn't have to wait too long. A sudden hammering on the door, and my heart was hammering in my chest.

"Police! Open up!"

Aaron's hands were trembling as he gingerly opened the door. Two uniformed police officers stepped inside.

"Aaron Bernhardt, Miriam Bernhardt, Joséphine Bernhardt. You are to accompany us to the station," said one of the officers as he read names from a clipboard.

"What's this about? We have done nothing wrong!" said Aaron.

"Just a formality. We need to verify your identification," the officer replied. "Now, come along."

"But I'm not Joséphine!" I said. "She's gone missing!"

The officer didn't seem too concerned. "You have to accompany us anyway. It won't take long." He gestured to one of the buses that were lined up along the street. "All you need are your papers. Quickly now!"

As the couple went to get their documents, I did my best to convince the officer he should let me go. "My name is Louise Bellingham. I work for the German Counterintelligence Bureau. You really should let me go."

"Mademoiselle," said the officer. "It's not my concern. You can sort it all out when we get to the station. I'm sure it will be easily resolved if you are telling the truth."

As we were ushered toward one of the trucks, I suddenly realized that everyone on the street had been ordered to leave their homes. I noticed women in nightgowns, some with young children, and realized this must be a raid.

The French police were rounding up Jewish families.

And I'd left my identification papers at home.

CHAPTER 26

Herded like reluctant cattle onto the bus, almost everyone had something to say.

"This is an outrage! Taken from our homes at this hour of the night!"

"They wouldn't even let me change out of my nightgown!"

"My children were fast asleep in bed. I had to wake them up!"

The policemen were reassuring. "Sorry, Madame. It's just a formality. We'll have you home soon!"

Miriam's thoughts were still of Joséphine. "What if she comes home while we're gone? I should have left a note!"

As the bus moved off, we passed a police barricade, evidently preventing anyone from leaving the area. My heart sank as I saw they weren't just being manned by Paris policemen. Germans were there, too, ostentatiously raising their rifles at the bus as we drove past. *Maybe they think we might make a run for it by jumping out of the windows,* I thought.

I found myself sitting next to a terrified-looking young woman with a crying baby in her arms. "I'm sorry," she said in my direction. "I wanted to change her diaper, but they wouldn't let me. She's crying because she's wet and uncomfortable."

"Please, don't apologize," I said. "She's cute. What's her name?"

"Angélique. She's six weeks old." Tears filled her eyes. "My husband wasn't home when they came—he works nights, you see. Where do you think they're taking us?"

I didn't know what to say. The whole thing seemed strange to me, and the story about having to simply check our identities didn't ring true. But, just then, like an answer to a prayer, the bus stopped.

"You will enter the police station in an orderly fashion and wait your turn," said the police officer from the front of the bus. The young woman turned to me and forced a smile. Perhaps they had been telling us the truth after all.

I stood in line with Miriam and Aaron, expecting the wait to be hours long. But it wasn't. We watched the families ahead of us move up to the counter, where their papers were rapidly checked by a French official. From there, most of them seemed to be directed back onto the bus, while others were sent to sit in a waiting area. When our turn came, I approached the counter with the Bernhardts, fully prepared to argue my case.

"Aaron and Miriam Bernhard," said the official, running his finger down a list, then checking off their names. "Joséphine?" he asked, looking at me over his spectacles.

"No, I'm not! My name is Louise Bellingham," I said.

"Papers, please?"

"I don't have them with me, but you can verify my..."

"Then where is Joséphine Bernhardt?" he interrupted.

"We don't know," said Aaron. "She went missing. I filed a report right here at this very police station today!"

The official momentarily stared at Aaron in disbelief, shook his head, and checked off Joséphine's name on his list. "To the bus!" he said.

Now it was my turn to look disbelieving. "To the bus? All of us?" I asked.

"Yes!" was the impatient reply.

I couldn't believe my luck. I was off the hook, about to be returned to the Bernhardts' house.

Or so I thought.

⋇

I sat myself next to the young woman with the crying baby again, by which time I figured it must have been close to one o'clock in the morning. The bus slowly filled up with tired-looking passengers, all believing that they were about to be taken home, and when the bus finally pulled away, there was a collective sigh of relief.

Until someone realized we were going in the wrong direction. "What's going on here? This isn't the way home? Where are you taking us?"

The guard standing at the front of the bus suddenly wasn't as reassuring as he had been before, especially when one of the men left his seat and started to walk toward him.

"SIT DOWN!" he commanded. When he pointed his rifle at the man, some of the women screamed, and a wave of terror washed over me. We had been lied to...we weren't going home. The word "camp" entered my head. There had been rumors of dreadful places where Jews were imprisoned in dreadful conditions, sometimes shot en masse. *Why would they call them camps?* I wondered distractedly. *Camps were supposed to be fun places where you slept in tents and went for hikes. I wish I was camping right now. Even in England. Even in the rain...*

To my surprise, the bus stopped. We had only been on the road for ten minutes or so and couldn't have even left the Paris suburbs in that short time. Once again, my hopes rose.

"I know this place," said a voice from behind. "Drancy. It was built as a housing complex for low-income families back in the 'thirties. But the rents were too high, and the workmanship was shoddy at best. Last I heard, they were using it as a detention center for British and French prisoners of war."

A subdued silence ensued as people digested this piece of information. We peered out of the bus windows in the moonlight to see several concrete towers and a glint of barbed wire.

"It can't be too bad if it was built for families to live in," I said to my companion, squeezing her hand. She looked at me gratefully and nodded while the baby, worn out from crying, emitted feeble little sobs.

We looked expectantly toward the front of the bus, expecting to be told to exit. The driver left, the guard stood with his rifle in hand, and we waited. And waited.

"Excuse me," said a shaky voice. An older lady had raised her hand to get the guard's attention. "I'm sorry, but I need the toilet. How long do we have to wait?"

"I don't know!" was the gruff response. He wouldn't even look at her, I noticed.

Children were crying, some of the women, too. When the door opened and the guard stepped out, we were hopeful once again. But a different guard—a younger man—took the old one's place, and once again, the door was closed.

"Please!" begged one of the men. "We've been waiting for hours with no toilets and nothing to eat or drink. Can we at least get off the bus and wait outside?"

It would have been a relief. My legs were starting to cramp up, and even though the bus windows were open, an unpleasant smell pervaded the vehicle.

"You're not allowed to exit until I get the order," said the young guard. At least he had the decency to look uncomfortable.

"How can you treat us like this?" insisted the same voice. "We're French citizens, just like you! Look at us, for God's sake! Do we look like the enemy to you?"

The guard did indeed look at us. He rubbed his forehead and squeezed the bridge of his nose. "I have my orders. I'm sorry," he said.

"I don't know how you can live with yourself," said someone else. A comment that he ignored.

The hours dragged by. Occasionally I dozed off, only to be awakened by coughs, cries, or loud, angry comments. My throat felt parched, my head ached, and I was sickened by the ever-worsening stench that clung to my hair and clothes. From time to time, I'd glance back at Miriam and Aaron, who were leaning into each other with their eyes closed. *Such a devoted couple,* I thought, wondering if Hans and I would be so close when we were that age.

Hans. A stirring of anger rose up from the pit of my stomach.

I pushed it aside.

As the night sky faded to shades of gray and a soft pink sunrise streaked across the horizon, my companions were starting to show their desperation. Voices became louder, demanding, strident.

"*Please!*" sobbed a woman. "If you have any humanity in you at all, please let us off this damned bus. *I can't take it anymore!*"

The guard looked almost fearful. "Just a minute," he said and disappeared off the bus. With that, people rose from their seats to stretch their legs, myself included. Through the window, I could see other buses lined up in front and behind us.

"Are you all right?" I asked the Bernhardts.

"Yes, thank you, ma petite," said Miriam with a smile.

Her daughter's gone missing, she's been torn from her home without being allowed to take any belongings, forced to line up in a police station, and then to sit in a bus for countless hours overnight. And she thanks me for asking if she was all right!

The guard returned.

"You can get off the bus now, but you must stay close," he said.

"Are there facilities with toilets?" someone asked.

"I don't know," he shrugged.

Stiff-legged and apprehensive, we descended from the bus onto a lawn surrounded by low shrubs and pathways. But when we looked up, we saw we were in a complex of dreary four-story buildings surrounded by a double barbed-wire fence. And just in case we were in any doubt as to whether or not we were prisoners, we needed only to glance up at the guards on platforms set high above the ground, rifles pointed directly at us.

Mothers were taking their children over to the far side of the lawn to relieve themselves. The low bushes provided no privacy, but soon the adults, myself included, were drifting over there for the same purpose. If they wanted to humiliate us, they couldn't have found a better way. But the ill-treatment was far from over.

By the time we were ordered to line up in front of the barbed wire, the heat from the sun was intense. I took this opportunity to plead my case.

"I shouldn't be here," I said to one of the guards. I lowered my voice. "I'm not even Jewish. It's a case of mistaken identity!"

"You'll get the chance to tell someone later," he replied. "Now, take your place by the fence!"

With not so much as a drop of water since last night and no sleep, some found it difficult to remain standing. Miriam sat down heavily on the concrete, with her husband standing close, trying to provide her with some shade from his body.

Why did everything always have to take so long? I wondered, feeling hot, thirsty, and light-headed.

"Soup!" somebody said excitedly. And sure enough, we were each handed a small tin cup of a weak and watery substance that was hardly recognizable as soup. What wouldn't I have given for a bowl of that turnip soup I used to despise so much. Finally, the line began to move at a snail's pace in the direction of one of the buildings. Not without its casualties, however. Ahead of us, an elderly woman lay flat on the ground, having evidently collapsed.

"Help! It's my mother! I think she's unconscious!"

The son kneeled next to his mother in despair. "She's not breathing! You've killed her!"

As one guard lifted the woman under her arms, another one took her legs, and she was carried toward the building. The son, naturally, made to go with her, but the guards weren't having that, and he was pushed back into line with the butt of a rifle.

"How could they be so cruel?" asked Aaron. "These are our countrymen. Why do they hate us so much?"

Once we got closer to the door, I could hear shouting and saw people passing in front of inspectors who were checking documents. *They have to believe me,* I thought, *even though I don't have identification with me. A simple telephone call to Hans is all that's needed. And surely, he must be so worried about me by now. He will certainly figure out what happened after he talks to my mother. He'll probably be here to get me any minute now.*

I looked around to see if there were any cars in the vicinity, but no. Even the buses were gone. It was a relief to enter the building, to get out of the intense glare of the sun. But then I realized what the shouting was about. They were separating families—men from the women, and worst of all, children from their parents. Tears coursed down my face as I watched two young children, who couldn't have been more than eight years old, physically forced away from their mother. Their cries of fear and outrage were excruciating.

Hans! How can you allow this suffering to take place?

Then, for the first time: *He's a monster.*

How could I have fallen for someone so evil?

Following close behind Miriam and a red-faced, sweating Aaron, I waited for the inevitable question.

"Joséphine Bernhardt?"

"No, I'm not. Listen, they took me by mistake..." On I rambled to a bored-looking bureaucrat about my real identity and who I worked for. "All you have to do is telephone the Counterintelligence Office, and they'll vouch for me. I can even give you the number."

"That won't be necessary, Mademoiselle. We'll look into it." He looked past me. "Next!"

"Wait!" I said. "You have no right to detain me! I'm not a French citizen, and I'm not Jewish. *I shouldn't be here!*"

"She's not Jewish, so she shouldn't be here?" said a woman's voice from behind me. "Well, isn't *she* special!"

"Mademoiselle!" said the clerk. "You have no papers! What exactly did you expect? Now, move along."

Shamefaced, I watched Aaron and Miriam look into each other's eyes and gently squeeze each other's hands before moving off in different directions. *That could never be Hans and I,* I realized. *How could I marry him now?*

As I followed Miriam and the rest of the women along the gloomy hallway, I prayed to be rescued. Hans may no longer be the man of my dreams, but I was still relying on him to get me out of this nightmare.

CHAPTER 27

We were led up a flight of stairs to an airless room furnished with a dozen or so bunk beds. There were no mattresses, just planks, with one filthy-looking woolen blanket on each bed.

"Two to each bed," said the guard. *Two to a bed?* These were narrow cots, hardly big enough for one, let alone two.

Some of the beds were already taken. I pointed out an empty lower bunk to Miriam, and we sat to claim it as our own. As other women arrived, the air in the room became increasingly oppressive, with an overpowering stench of sweat. None of us had any personal possessions with us, not even toiletry items, I realized.

There was a bathroom across the hall, the guard announced before backing out of the room when every bed was taken.

"You go," I said to Miriam. "I'll make sure no one takes our bed."

I lay back on the planks listening to the voices around me.

"How can two of us sleep in such a small space?"

"Even if I did get to sleep, I'd be afraid of falling off and hurting myself."

"What do you think they're going to do with us?"

What indeed? If they planned to have us all shot, wouldn't they have done so already? Why go to all the trouble of putting us here otherwise? My best guess was that this was just a place to put us before we were transported elsewhere. *Out of the country? Germany, perhaps?*

Miriam was gone a long time. She came back looking dispirited, telling me there was a queue.

Of course there's a queue. There's always a queue, I grumbled to myself as I waited my turn with a rifle pointing in my direction. After a ten-minute wait, I entered the bathroom to find three toilet stalls and a row of sinks. A mere trickle of water emerged as women desperately tried to turn on the taps. There was no toilet paper. The toilet I used was no longer flushing, looking dangerously close to overflowing.

"The toilets are overflowing, and there's no water," I called to the guard when I emerged. "You need to send a plumber!"

He shrugged. "Yes, we know," he said, as if bored.

"I don't think you understand," I pressed on. "If we can't even wash our hands…why, there are diseases…"

"That's a shame," he said, leaning back against the wall with a smirk.

It felt like a slap across the face, the last straw. Every muscle in my body tensed up, my chest felt tight, and I was breathing like a raging bull.

"You heartless bastard!" I screamed. "You call yourself a French citizen? These women are just as French as you are! Whose side are you on?"

Whose side are you on? Didn't someone ask me the same question not that long ago?

The soldier raised his rifle and started angrily toward me. "Hey, I'm following orders, you Jewish slut! Someone needs to teach you a lesson!" He raised the butt of his rifle as I instinctively cried out, putting my hands over my head as I stumbled backward and fell to my knees.

But the blow never came.

"Soldier!" said a voice. "Attention!"

My would-be attacker had been stopped in his tracks by an apparently superior officer. "Louise Bellingham?" he asked, studying me with aversion.

"Yes," I croaked, staggering to my feet and trying to control my breathing.

"Thought so. You're to follow me. As you were!" he said over his shoulder to the guard.

As you were? …in other words, feel free to beat up any of these defenseless women if they should offend you in any way?

I followed along down the stairs and then into an office area. How pleasantly cool and fresh the air down here felt in comparison to upstairs.

It has to be Hans. He's come for me at last.

I heard the name Hartmann, and with a sense of relief that it must be all over, I was shown into a room empty but for a table and chairs. I'd barely sat down when the door opened, and I turned expectantly with a smile on my face. As yet, I had no idea how I would end our relationship, but it was important for Hans to think I was pleased to see him. I didn't want him to leave me here, after all.

My smile must have slipped.

"Ah, Louise!" he chuckled. "I'm not who you were quite expecting, obviously!"

The General.

I tried to recover myself. "General! How good to see you. I hope you're here to rescue me!"

"I heard of your…shall we say…*predicament* and thought it might be the perfect opportunity for us to…chat!"

Ugh, he gives me the creeps. "Chat?"

"Yes, chat. While I have you as a captive audience, as it were."

He seemed to think this was highly amusing, laughing appreciatively at his own joke. I laughed too. Not easy to do when you're terrified out of your wits.

"You see, Louise…" He sat across the table and gazed at me intently. "I know exactly who you are."

Oh, no. He knows either about New Year's Eve or that I'm the killer they've been searching for.

"In fact, I probably know more about you than you know about yourself!"

I braced myself for the accusation to come, determining to deny everything.

He folded his plump white hands on the table, displaying ornate rings on both hands, including one fashioned in the shape of a swastika. Vividly recalling the feeling of that hand on my knee, I suppressed a shudder.

"You see, when my nephew brought you into the fold, as it were, I did some investigating into you and your family. I remembered the name. Bellingham, but couldn't quite put my finger on it at first. Then it all fell into place."

He was speaking in riddles, as far as I was concerned.

"Your father."

Now he had my full attention.

"You were actually there when he was murdered. Am I right?"

I nodded.

"But you never found out who actually killed him, did you?"

I felt the blood drain out of my face. "No."

"Then allow me to enlighten you. But first of all, you need to understand who your father really was. He was a menace, a threat to the Third Reich, an instigator. He insisted on speaking out against the Fuhrer at a time when public opinion was so important. Your father planted lies and seeds of doubt in the minds of many important men. And governments!"

The General stood up and paced up and down the room as his face turned red, and his voice rose in anger.

"We warned him, let me tell you! We told him to desist. To stop the slander. But he wouldn't. In the end, we had no choice…"

I looked at him in horror. "You…?

"Oh, no, not *me!* My brother. Hans' father. He was the one who gave the order. He didn't actually pull the trigger, you understand. But he gave the order."

Hans' father was responsible for my father's assassination. My mind reeled. I was speechless.

General Hartmann sat back down at the table. "Hans doesn't know about this, by the way. I didn't want to tell him. He's so fond of you, you see. Thinks you have a future together. I really don't know how he'll react when he finds out…"

"Are you going to tell him?" I asked faintly.

"No, no. I'll leave that decision to you, my dear. I see it as a true test of your allegiance. If you are as dedicated to the Nazi cause as Hans seems to think you are, you'll have no problem accepting the fact that your father was a menace and deserved to die."

He rose from his seat again and made to move toward the door.

"Oh, and one more thing," he said, turning to face me. "Your mother. Turns out she's just as reckless as your father. She's been working for the Resistance."

My sharp intake of breath led him to believe I was surprised.

"I'm afraid I'm overloading you," he said. "But you need to know. I've spoken to her, and we came to an agreement. She's working for us now. In exchange for information about the Resistance, we will spare the life of her son. Your brother. So far, she's been most helpful."

I was in shock. Numb. Unable to think through all that he had told me. When the door opened, and Hans appeared, I looked at him blankly.

"What's going on?" Hans asked, looking from me to his uncle.

"Ah, my boy. Perfect timing! We were just having a lovely little chat," said the General. "About family!" He slapped his nephew playfully on the back and left the room, chuckling to himself.

�▽

"My poor darling!" said Hans, holding his arms out to me.

I put up my hand. "No, don't come near me. I stink to high heaven, and I don't want your uniform to get soiled."

He took a step back.

"My precious girl! I only just found out where you were! What a horrible experience for you, being locked up with that scum all night."

By "that scum," he means Jews. Sweet Miriam, kind-hearted Aaron, the lovely young woman with the baby.

"I can't believe what they were thinking when they took you. Typical French inefficiency!"

Oh, you'd be surprised at how efficient they were, I thought. If the goal is to round up as many Jews as possible and make their lives a living hell, the French police are doing a pretty good job.

"You look so pale. My driver will take you home. I'll stick around here for a while with Uncle to see how things are going. Overall, the operation was a huge success, apparently. Four thousand Jews in one night!"

He caught the expression on my face.

"I'm sorry, I shouldn't have said it was a success. Not with you caught in the middle! Come along. Let's get you to the car."

Leaning my weary head against the back of the seat as the car pulled away, I stared at the windows of the second floor where Miriam and the other women were imprisoned. The floodgates opened, and the tears came accompanied by huge, gasping sobs. The inhumanity of it all, the barbarity, the cruelty.

I will do everything I can to get you out of there, I promise. This is my war now, and I know what side I'm on.

CHAPTER 28

I hadn't expected Maman to be home. But as soon as I opened
the door, there she was.

"Thank goodness! I was so worried about you!"

She stepped toward me as if to give me a hug, but I held
out my hand to stop her as I had with Hans. "No, I smell really
bad," I said.

"As if I care about that!" she said and wrapped her arms
around me anyway. Which set off my tears all over again.
"When you didn't come back from Miriam's, I finally went
over there myself to see if you'd even arrived. I knew that you'd
left your papers here, so I was worried you'd been arrested."

She stepped back and looked me up and down in concern.
"When I got to their street, I saw a few people standing there
talking. I went up to them, and they told me there'd been a raid
and that everyone had been taken away in buses. One man was
almost crying because his wife and baby had been taken."

"Oh, Maman! It was so terrible!"

"I came back home and waited and waited. Then this morning, I decided the best thing to do would be to go and speak to your Captain Hartmann."

"Not *my* Captain Hartmann anymore," I said. "But thank you—it's because of him that I'm back home."

Half an hour later, I had washed and changed and was sitting at the kitchen table with the inevitable bowl of turnip soup and a piece of stale bread while Jacques watched. *Never again will I complain about turnip soup,* I thought. *Just to have food, any food, is a blessing.*

"I don't know what to tell you first," I said to Maman.

"What about Miriam and Aaron?" she asked. "Are they all right?"

"No," I said, fighting back tears. "They're not all right. Not at all. But first, I need to tell you what General Hartmann said to me."

"Oh." Her face turned pale, and she sat down heavily, avoiding my eyes. "Jacques, why don't you go and put the radio on in the sitting room?"

Jacques obediently left the room.

"Go on, then," she said with a sigh.

"He told me the truth about my father. And he told me who murdered him. Did you know?"

"Yes, he told me, too. When you first started going out with Hans."

"Why didn't you tell me?" I asked wearily. I didn't have the strength to get annoyed with her.

"Because you'd get angry. And upset. You would have accused me of trying to ruin your happiness."

Much as I hated to admit it to myself, she was right. That's exactly how I would have behaved. And I wasn't proud of it.

"The General told me something else too." I put down my soup spoon. "You're an informant. Giving the Nazis information about the Resistance."

Now it was her turn to cry. "He threatened me with Jacques! Said he'd take him away if I didn't cooperate. I'm so sorry, but he left me with no choice!" She looked at me imploringly. "I always protected you, Louise. I told him that you would have nothing to do with the Resistance, and I think he believed me. But I had to give him some real information, otherwise..." She looked toward the sitting room.

"You told him about Joséphine?" I asked.

"Yes, it was me who gave her up!" She put her head into her hands and sobbed. "He already knew about her—I'm sure of that—and he was putting me to the test. I had to tell him the truth!"

"Oh, Maman. I'm so sorry!"

We both stood up at the same time and held onto each other while we cried. My mother and I were bonding for the first time, for all the wrong reasons, with tears instead of smiles. Tears of sorrow, tears of regret, tears of utter anguish.

"Don't worry," I told her. "We'll find a way to save Joséphine. Miriam and Aaron, too!" *We have to. How can I live with myself otherwise?*

⸙

We sat together for hours that evening, talking without argument or recriminations for the first time I could remember. I told her how the Jewish families on the Bernhardts' street had been rounded up, about how they hadn't been allowed to bring any belongings with them, about the journey to the police station, and then on to Drancy. I described how we'd been confined to the bus overnight, told her about how families were separated, then spoke of the horrendous living and sleeping conditions inside the building.

"You must write it all down while it's fresh in your memory," she said at one point. "We must let the world know what's going on."

"I will," I replied. "We can publish it in your newspaper to start."

"Do you think that Hans would get the Bernhardts released if you asked him?" she wanted to know. "If you told him how much it would mean to you?"

"Not a hope," I said. "It's as if his hatred for Jews is the most important thing in his life. He's obsessed. Anyway, I don't want him to lose his trust in me. I'm sure that somehow, I can use him to our advantage. I just haven't figured out how, as yet."

I was just about to mention that I wanted to talk to Claude when the doorbell rang. I followed Maman to the hall as she opened the door. It wasn't Claude, though. It was Hans…so tall, so handsome, radiating health and vitality, and looking very pleased with himself.

"Ah, Madame. I just wanted to check on Louise after her dreadful experience!"

My mother played her part well. "Captain Hartmann! Of course, please come in. And thank you for rescuing my daughter!"

"My pleasure," he said with a stiff little bow. "Louise, there you are! How are you feeling?"

Sick at heart; appalled by all that I saw; incensed that the French police could be so callous toward their own countrymen; distressed by man's inhumanity to man. Not to mention deeply ashamed of my own selfish behavior and my unwillingness to see you for who you really are.

"I'm fine," I said. "Just tired, that's all."

Maman disappeared into the sitting room to give us some privacy, and he took me into his arms for a kiss. He was still in uniform; I was repelled by the sight of it; all I wanted to do was push him away in disgust, but that wouldn't have helped the Bernhardts. So, I kissed him back, then yawned.

"I'll leave you to go to bed," he said. "Sleep tight, and take tomorrow off to rest if you need it."

"Thank you. You're so good to me," I said. "But I'm sure I'll be there!"

He nodded happily, and as I closed the door after him, I let out a sigh of relief. He hadn't yet asked me what I was doing at the Bernhardts' house at such a late hour. I would need to come up with a convincing excuse, but not at that moment. Exhaustion washed over me, and after a hug for Maman, I sank gratefully into my bed. I must have immediately fallen into a deep sleep but woke myself up to the sound of my own screams in the early hours of the morning. What the nightmare had been about, I couldn't recall, but my thoughts immediately drifted to Miriam, who was living a nightmare from which she couldn't awake. What must she have thought when I didn't return? What about the toilets that had been almost overflowing when I left? The lack of running water and food? Had she been forced to share the bunk with another woman, someone she didn't know? How could anyone expect to sleep in such conditions?

I have to get her out of there.

Then there was Joséphine, who we presumed had been arrested for being part of the Resistance. She would have been taken to German Counterintelligence Headquarters—the dreaded building on Avenue Foch, which was rapidly becoming known as the "Street of Horrors."

Blocking out the images that came to mind, I got out of bed and wandered around downstairs, figuring out what to do.

I smiled to myself as I imagined a thousand-strong army of resisters. With armored tanks, on white horses, with machine guns and swords, we'd storm first Drancy, then Avenue Foch, releasing hoards of prisoners and driving out the Nazis. Every last one of them. Back along the Champs-Elysees, all the way back to Germany.

Including Hans.

But that wasn't the least bit realistic. Not only were we abysmally short of men because they'd all gone off to war, we also had no weapons. *Still, I have to do something.* My father's favorite quote echoed in my head.

"All that is necessary for the triumph of evil is that good men do nothing."

I might not have weapons, but I certainly have my wits. If Hans loves and trusts me enough, there has to be some way for me to trick him into doing what I want.

My mother's suggestion of simply pleading for their release wasn't going to work; I needed to be smarter than that. And I wasn't going to be able to pull it off on my own, I realized. Tomorrow, I would start reaching out to the people I'd hurt.

I needed my friends back.

CHAPTER 29

The next morning, I paid particular attention to my appearance and made sure I was on time for work. But I had a job to do first. Before taking the elevator, I stood for a moment at the entrance to the bar and looked around. Just as I had hoped, there was no one in sight. As quickly as I could, I went behind the bar, praying that the mail slot was still there. It was; I slipped my note inside.

Help, please, it read.

My hands started to sweat as I walked away, trying not to look suspicious. I was taking a tremendous risk here—not knowing if Claude was still around, if he'd been captured, or if, indeed, the mail slot itself had been compromised. *I have to be prepared to take risks,* I told myself. *Otherwise, I won't accomplish anything.*

Hans greeted me with enthusiasm in the office, enquiring solicitously about my health and insisting that we go out for dinner that evening. This fell perfectly in with my plans.

"That would be lovely, thank you! You're too good to me! Can you pick me up at the house? I know Maman would like to see you, if only for a minute or so."

This was the first time I'd asked him to pick me up at home, and it was easy to see how flattered he was. *He has such an ego,* I thought. *I don't know why I didn't see it before.*

Looking equally as smug, the General soon made an appearance when he saw I was alone. I knew he was fishing. He wanted to know what I was going to do about the revelations he'd made about my father. After he had finished gushing and asking me how I was, I went in for the attack.

"I'm fine, really, General. And I wanted to thank you for telling me the truth about my father. I always suspected something was amiss there, but now I know. Between you and I," I lowered my voice, and he leaned forward in anticipation, "This is one secret that I won't be sharing with Hans. I don't want anything to come between the two of us."

"Splendid, splendid! Delighted to hear it, my dear, and I couldn't agree more!"

His tone may have been jovial, but his eyes were cold. I knew I could never trust him.

In an effort to stop thinking about the Bernhardts, I threw myself into my work but with a different mindset. Surreptitiously changing or omitting names and addresses, I made small amendments to a few of the letters that passed over my desk. Not so many that my interference might have been detected, but enough to potentially save a few Jews from being arrested. In addition, a formal document from Germany mysteriously disappeared—with a little help from me—when I read over its contents. More antisemitic laws along with harsher punishments really weren't necessary, I decided.

I knew that my efforts may only have temporary results, but nonetheless, it felt good to be doing something.

When Hans stopped in to take me to lunch, I gracefully declined.

"I'm working through my lunch hour," I told him. "I'll just eat a sandwich at my desk. I'd like to leave a little earlier than usual today, if you don't mind."

He didn't.

By four o'clock, I was becoming agitated. After two days of being held at Drancy, I dreaded thinking how Aaron and Miriam must be feeling. And as for Joséphine, I couldn't even bear to think about what she must be going through. But now was the time for me to take action. My first stop on my way out was the bar, mercifully empty except for a single officer drinking alone at one of the tables and Sacha behind the bar, drying glasses.

He looked deliberately away from me as I approached, trying to ignore me.

"I've come to apologize," I said in a low voice. "You were right. I should never have got involved with him."

"Hmph," said Sacha with a toss of the head as if to say I told you so.

"I'm trying to make amends," I said.

"Are you looking for a round of applause?"

I couldn't help but smile. "That would be nice. But, umm, do you mind if I just pop behind the bar for a second? I think I left something here." My eyes slid in the direction of the mail slot.

Another huge risk, I thought. *How do I know that Sacha isn't working for the Germans?*

"Please yourself," he said and carried on nonchalantly with his drying while I scurried around to the slot. It was empty.

"Thanks, Sacha. I'll buy you a drink sometime!" I hurried out of the bar feeling his eyes boring into my back.

Someone had taken my message. But had it ended up in the right hands? That was the question. Cycling my way through the city streets, I headed for my next destination, Emma's aunt's house. It was time for me to make another apology.

She opened the door and looked at me questioningly.

"Emma, I'm sorry!" I blurted. "I've been a real idiot. Can you ever forgive me?"

"Come in," she said after a moment's hesitation. But then she gave me a lopsided smile. "Tell me all, then I'll decide whether to forgive you or not!"

We sat in her aunt's stuffy sitting room with a pot of tea while I poured my heart out. "I was hopelessly in love with him and just wanted to believe he was perfect. When he talked about Jews with such hatred, I brushed it aside. I kept thinking, oh well, after the war's over and after we're married, all this talk of Jews will go away, and then we'll be happy."

Without going into too much detail, I told her about my experience at Drancy. "I have to do something to help those poor people. I have half a plan but hope to meet up later with someone who might help me. In the meantime, I'm keeping Hans close without letting on that I've had a change of heart."

"Louise," said Emma. "I was planning on going back to England soon. But if there's anything I can do to help… anything at all…let me know."

"How much of a risk would you be willing to take?" I asked. "Would you put yourself in danger? Because that's what I'd be asking."

"I would," she said. "We need to stand up to these bullies. Count me in!"

\\//

I cycled home as fast as I could, let myself in through the front door, and called out for Jacques. With Miriam gone, Maman had decided that he would have to stay at home on his own while we were both at work.

"He knows the rules. He's not to leave the house or answer the front door if anyone comes. I'll leave him something for his lunch, and he has all his toys to play with. And he knows how to turn on the radio if he gets bored. Really, I have no other choice!"

Having promised to take him out to the park when I got home, I was fully expecting him to be waiting for me anxiously with his toy boat in hand. But there was no sign of him. Calling his name, I swept through the entire house, looking in all his usual hiding places.

Then started to panic.

They've taken him! They found the message I left at the bar and knew it must have come from me. Maybe Sacha betrayed me. Oh, why was I so stupid? What a terrible mistake. They know I'm trying to contact the Resistance. My game is up!

I tried to reason with myself, thinking perhaps he'd gone outside for a walk. But Jacques would never do that on his own; he was too scared. Then I remembered the time he'd hidden from me before. *How could I forget? He has a hiding place that I don't know about!*

In an effort to coax him out, I stood in the front hall and sang to him.

Frère Jacques, Frère Jacques.
We're going to the park; we're going to the park!

Within seconds, there he was beside me, grinning from ear to ear and holding his boat out in front of him. A wave of relief swept over me.

"Don't ever do that again!" I said with tears in my eyes, wrapping my arms around him. "That was a cruel trick!"

Sitting on a bench at the park, watching Jacques, I wondered how long it would take Claude to contact me. If he ever did, that is. Why didn't I say in the message how urgently I needed his help? A matter of life and death. *How long can any of the Bernhardts be expected to survive in such brutal conditions?* But then, when a man with a dog sat down at the other end of the bench, I didn't think anything of it until he spoke.

"Don't look at me," he said.

I froze; held my breath.

"Go to the Mirabel Bookstore. Ask for the works of Shakespeare."

I waited, but as I watched out of the corner of my eye, he patted his dog and went on his way. He hadn't told me a time, I realized. Also, it could be a set-up designed to lure me in to be arrested. Regardless, I had no choice but to hope for the best and go to the bookstore.

I forced myself to sit at the park for a few more minutes to allow Jacques more time at the lake and so as not to appear suspicious to anyone following me. It was more than likely that the General was having both me and my mother followed, I reasoned, so I needed to be cautious. Jacques and I ambled home as if without a care in the world, and much to my relief, Maman was home when we returned. I told her about the exchange at the park and set out on my own as if going shopping, basket in hand.

On this summer's afternoon, there were plenty of people walking the streets. Every now and again, I would stop to look in a shop window while scanning the street behind me. I didn't see anyone suspicious but figured that it would be easy to outsmart someone like me, who had no experience in the spy business. I bought a tiny piece of beef at the butcher's, which we would use for soup, and was lucky enough to get a loaf of bread at the bakery. From there, I made my way into the bookstore, looking out at the street through the window for a minute in case anyone followed me in.

A bearded young man was watching me from behind the counter in an otherwise empty store.

"I'm looking for the works of Shakespeare," I said.

"Follow me," he said in response, leading me to the back of the shop to a flight of stairs. "Up there!" He turned and left while I nervously navigated the stairs to find Claude waiting for me at the top.

"Thank goodness it's you!" I said. "This is hard on the nerves."

"You get used to it after a while," he said. "Do you think you were followed?"

"I don't think so," I said. "I wouldn't have come in if I'd thought I was."

We were in a large, open room, which seemed to be mostly used for storage. Claude went over to the window and peered through the blinds for a minute, then indicated a couple of chairs.

"Sit, and tell me what's going on. You shouldn't stay here too long."

I wasted no time in telling him everything. I wasn't sure how much he knew, so I omitted nothing. It was one thing telling my friend Emma about my relationship with Hans but quite another explaining it to this older man, whose penetrating stare made me feel weak, irresponsible, and impetuous. Not to mention shallow. But he didn't react or make any comments—not until I told him about my mother's betrayal, that is. At that point, he groaned as if in pain and stood up.

After checking the street again, Claude returned to his seat.

"What do you want me to do? Why are you here?" His voice was brusque, abrupt.

"I'm in a position of power with Captain Hartmann," I said. "I think I can get him to arrange the release of both Joséphine and her parents if I go about it the right way. But I need to know that you can get all three of them out of danger—either into the free zone or out of the country—if I succeed."

"Possibly," he said. "Presuming Joséphine is still alive, that is."

"I know," I said. "That's why I need to act fast. Now here's my plan..."

CHAPTER 30

That night, over dinner with Hans, I talked about frivolous things—a dress I'd seen in the window of a shop on the Champs-Élysées, a just-released movie that I'd like to go and see, how hot the weather had been of late. I told him an amusing story about Ingrid, the typist, whose hiccoughs, to her acute embarrassment, had lasted for a full hour. I pretended to be drinking as much wine as I normally would, even tipping a full glass of wine into a handy plant pot while his attention was elsewhere.

This was the Louise he'd fallen for—fun-loving, unpredictable, entertaining, and never too serious. No matter how I felt inside, I had to keep up the act.

"Oh, by the way," I sloshed some of my wine into my dessert. "Whoops! Oh, dear!"

Hans laughed, watching me with affection.

"Where was I? Oh, yes, I have some information for you. Or for the General, if you like."

"Information?" he asked, staring at me intently.

"Yes. There was a massive escape route being planned. For Jews. All the way from Paris to Spain."

"Really! How did you find out about it?"

"I heard them talking about it. Could we have our coffee now?"

"Of course, darling." Hans clicked his fingers at the waiter. "*Who* was talking about it?"

The waiter arrived at the table.

"Coffee!" said Hans to him impatiently. He was always so pompous and ill-mannered with anyone he considered to be beneath him. Which was practically everyone.

"Joséphine Bernhardt and her parents. They're the masterminds behind it. But then Joséphine was arrested, and her parents were taken to Drancy, so the whole thing fell through."

"But that's a good thing, then—that it fell through," said Hans with a smile.

"No, I don't think so! Imagine if it *had* been set up! Imagine all those arrests you could have made…all those names, and all those locations that could have been raided. Farms, attics, and abandoned buildings, mostly, from what I understand. And there are people making forged identity cards, too. All the way from here to Spain—it would have been quite a coup!"

I let that sink in for a minute as Hans looked thoughtful.

"Oh, good, here's our coffee," I said.

"You know," I continued. "It's too bad they were arrested. Otherwise, I might have been able to get all the information and pass it on to you. Or your uncle, of course."

"Are you saying you think they would share this information with you? Willingly?"

"Of course they would! They used to work for my mother, so they know me." I giggled. "Or they think they do, anyway!"

We went for our usual after-dinner stroll along the riverbank, and I bided my time, waiting for the right opportunity.

"We were meant for each other, you and I," said Hans, his arm around my waist as we sauntered along. "Destined to be together."

"We were," I agreed. "We make a good team!" Then, as if inspired by a sudden idea. "Why don't we make it happen? This escape route? All you'd have to do is get the Bernhardts released, and I'd look after the rest."

"Release them?" he asked with a frown.

"Yes, just the three of them, for a while. Then when I have the list of names and places, you'll be able to arrest not just them but dozens of other traitors, if not hundreds."

"Hmm, maybe I'll talk to my uncle about it."

"You could. Or you could do it all on your own, without him. I don't know how it works, but I'm sure something as big as this would earn you a lot of praise. Maybe even a promotion!" I stopped myself there, hoping I hadn't pushed too far.

"Possibly." He seemed lost in thought.

"I always knew you were the handsomest and smartest man in the German army!" I said, standing on tiptoe to kiss him on the cheek.

"Shall we go back to the hotel for a nightcap?" he asked, as I knew he would.

"I'd rather you drop me off at home if you don't mind," I said. "I'm still trying to recover from my dreadful experience at Drancy."

It was the only truthful thing I'd said to him all night.

Time passed slowly the following morning at work. By noon, Hans hadn't mentioned anything about my idea, and I sank deeper and deeper into despondency, thinking he must have rejected the plan as being unworkable or too risky. I didn't want to bring up the subject again for fear of seeming too eager, so I held my tongue and waited, inwardly fretting about how much time was passing.

Faking a cheerful demeanor, I joined him for lunch in the hotel dining room, pretending to enjoy the sausages that he had ordered for me. All the while, I smiled and nodded as he talked about the Jewish round-ups. Thousands of people were being taken from their homes, their places of work, and even the streets, to be transported to concentration camps.

"Where are these camps?" I asked casually as I took a sip of wine.

"We have quite a large number of them here in France," said Hans proudly. "And more in Poland. The plan is to transport as many as possible into Poland by train."

"Ah. Very efficient," I said.

"The French would be wise to emulate our efficiency," he said. "But evidently, they don't have the intelligence. Where *did* that waitress disappear to?"

As I looked at him across the table, I no longer saw the handsome hero. All I could see now was a narrow-minded, intolerant bigot, an ignorant man full of rage and hate who believed himself to be superior to most other men, someone to whom violence—even against women—was second nature.

"What you were talking about last night…"

My heart skipped a beat, but I continued the pretense. "What was that?"

"About getting information about an escape route to Spain. Do you think you could carry it off?"

"Oh, that! Yes, of course—as long as the Bernhardts are released. I'd just play along with them, pretending to be on their side, all the while gathering information for you. It would be fun!"

My heart was pounding so hard I was afraid Hans would hear it.

"Then I think it might be worth a try," he said. "But I won't get Uncle involved. I do have the authority, and I'd like it to be my doing. If it all goes according to plan, I think he'll be very proud of me!"

"Of course he will!" I said dotingly.

This was exactly what I'd hoped for. The General was too suspicious—I didn't want him involved because he'd be asking too many questions. I desperately wanted to ask Hans how soon the Bernhardts could be released, but again, didn't want to appear too concerned. So I chatted away about inconsequential things until Hans decided it was time to go back to work.

"I'll be up there shortly," I said. "I just need to powder my nose."

In the ladies' room, I penned a cryptic note for Claude to let him know that the plan was in motion and headed to the bar. To my dismay, the new bartender—my replacement—watched me approach. Bold as brass, I smiled at him and went behind the bar, bending down as if to retrieve something from the bottom shelf as I put my note in the slot.

"Aha!" I said triumphantly, holding up my set of keys. "I knew they'd be here!"

The bartender smiled back at me and shrugged while I couldn't help but think how foolhardy I was being. *He could easily be a German spy. In which case, he would know I just placed a note in the slot. No one can be trusted these days—I have to be more careful!*

Later that afternoon, I came to the conclusion that it wouldn't seem too odd for me to want to know about the timing of the releases after all. Hans wasn't in his office, however, and it was almost time for me to go home when he came back.

"Everything is in order," he said. "I made a personal visit to both Drancy and Avenue Foch, and the prisoners are being released at my request."

I could have fainted from relief. It all seemed too good to be true. But there was still a lot to do, I reminded myself. Even if they made it home safely, they could easily be picked up and arrested again.

And so could I.

∿

"But how will they get home?" my mother wanted to know. "Will they just be kicked out onto the street?"

I raced home quickly, anxious to tell my mother the thrilling news. The same question had been bothering me too. It just didn't seem likely that either Joséphine or her parents would be driven home. And I couldn't imagine that any one of them would be in good enough health to walk any distance.

We packed what little food we had into a bag, and Maman, Jacques, and I walked to Miriam's house. We were prepared to wait for them as long as it took. As we approached their street, I felt my anxiety rising. *What if there's another raid? What if we're all taken, Jacques and Maman included? How could I possibly get us out of that predicament?* I felt so scared by the time we stood outside their house that I could barely make myself walk up to the front door.

Maman pulled out the key from under the mat at the front door and allowed Jacques and me to enter. As I took the bag of food into the kitchen, I stopped dead in my tracks. Sitting at the kitchen table were three terrified, gaunt-looking figures.

None of whom looked particularly pleased to see me.

CHAPTER 31

Joséphine stood up from the table, her face twisted with rage. "How *dare* you...how *dare* you come here after what you did!" she spat at me.

Her dark hair hung greasily from her head, black rings circled her eyes, her pale face streaked with dirt. "I think you should go!" she said, pointing at the door with a trembling hand.

Miriam and Aaron stared at me reproachfully without saying a word. Both of them looked as if they had aged ten years over the last few days, utter and complete exhaustion etched into their faces.

Maman walked around me to confront them. "Dear Lord," she said. "What have they done to you?"

Miriam moaned softly while Aaron put his hand on hers, and Joséphine defiantly wiped tears from her eyes.

"Louise had nothing to do with you being taken," said Maman to Joséphine. "It was..."

She was about to confess. *"Maman! No!"* I blurted. I didn't see the point in telling them the truth; it would only create more anger. I was about to say more when a knock at the back door paralyzed us all with fear.

"Oh, no," Miriam whimpered.

"Don't answer it," said Maman.

The knock came again, more insistently this time, and a voice called my name. "Louise, it's me." With a sigh of relief, I went to the door to let Claude in. He entered the kitchen and stopped dead in his tracks to look my mother straight in the eye.

This was the first time they'd met since he'd found out about her betrayal.

"Claude," said Joséphine, but he held up his hand as if to stop her talking and continued to look at Maman.

For several seconds, neither of them spoke.

Maman was the first one to break eye contact. "It couldn't be helped," she whispered, glancing over at Jacques.

He stared at her for a moment longer, then nodded and looked away himself. Suddenly I felt I could breathe again. Then, taking in the condition of the three people sitting at the table, Claude began to take charge of the situation.

"Louise and Margarite, can you prepare them some food?" he asked. "I have to tell them what they need to know."

"But…" Joséphine was obviously still angry, confused, and wanting answers.

"Joséphine, you and your parents are going to be smuggled out of Paris. For this, you have Louise to thank, but we're not going to go into that right now. We have to get you prepared."

Joséphine opened her mouth as if to speak but then sank back in her seat under Claude's scrutiny and nodded in compliance. As I sliced the bread while Maman heated up leftover soup, I listened to what he was saying.

"First, you will eat, then you will sleep. Before you go to bed, pack a few clothes in a single bag that you can easily carry. Make sure to put in a warm sweater or a jacket. You won't need your documents—you'll be getting new ones. You'll be leaving just before dawn, but I'll be here to make sure you're up and ready to go."

"Where are we going?" asked Aaron.

"Somewhere safe. That's all I can tell you for now."

They talked for a few minutes as Claude did his best to calm their fears. Once Maman and I had set out the food, Claude told us we should go home.

"Come to the bookstore tomorrow after work, Louise, and I'll have that information for you," he said. I knew he was referring to the false information I was to pass on to Hans, and a little shiver of anxiety passed through me.

We said hasty goodbyes to the Bernhardts, and it wasn't until we were partway home that I realized we might never see them again. If all went according to plan, that is. Both Maman and I were deep in our own thoughts when Jacques stopped walking and frowned.

"What happened to them?" he asked when we turned around to look at him questioningly.

I think Maman was as surprised as I. Jacques didn't usually ask questions like this. If he was upset by something, he would cry or hide, but rarely would he express himself in words.

Maman took his hand, glancing at me in anguish. "Do you mean Joséphine and her parents?"

He nodded.

"They were put in prison. But they shouldn't have been because they did nothing wrong."

"Did the Germans put them there?"

"Yes. The Nazis did," said Maman.

"Oh," said Jacques, continuing to walk, seemingly satisfied by the answer he'd been given.

It was an odd moment.

∿

The following morning at work, Hans was eager for information. "Did you see them? Did you speak to them? Any information as yet?"

"Hans," I said. "They've been imprisoned and starved for the past few days. It's not as if they can jump right back into what they were doing before. I have to give them time."

"Oh. Well, don't give them too much time. I don't want them escaping on me."

He was so cold and callous. So insensitive.

"Don't worry, I won't let that happen," I said. "I'll go and talk to them later and see what I can find out."

"Do that. Please. And take time off from the office here if you need to. This is important. I want to act quickly."

After falsifying a few letters and documents that morning, I did leave the office early. Not to see the Bernhardts, however, whom I hoped would be well out of Paris by now. I needed to arrange a few things. I fully expected Hans to act immediately once he'd received Claude's list of fabricated names and locations. Knowing him as well as I did, I knew he would get on the telephone to various military units, demanding that they send out contingents to raid these imaginary places, with the aim of making as many arrests as possible.

It would probably take a few hours afterward for Hans to find out that he'd been set up. But I wanted to make sure that the General wasn't around while his nephew was making the calls. The older, more experienced, ever-suspicious General was likely to put a halt to the operation, and once he found out that I was behind it all, I shuddered to think what he might do.

General Hartmann needed to be out of the picture for a while, and who better to help me with that than my dear friend Emma. I headed over to her aunt's house and told her my plan, to which she was most agreeable.

"Would you like me to stab him through the heart afterward, too?" she joked. "Oh, wait, I forgot—he doesn't have one!"

"Good Lord, please don't do that," I replied.

I didn't want Emma involved in any wrongdoing but had to admit to myself that the thought of "doing away" with the General had occurred to me more than once. *It's not as if you haven't killed one of them before*, a wicked little voice in my head whispered. And as Claude pointed out to me later, wouldn't he soon be demanding my arrest once he'd discovered what I'd done? But, evil as he was, how could I murder him, or indeed anyone, in cold blood?

At the bookstore, I was assured that the Bernhardts had made their getaway without a hitch, although Claude wouldn't tell me where they were headed. Then, after checking the street below through the blinds, he handed me a list of names, addresses, and places.

"I suggest you copy them down in your own handwriting," he said. "Make it look as if you were in a hurry."

I started writing, using my own pencil on the pages of a small diary I always carried around with me.

"None of these people actually exist," said Claude. "And neither do the addresses or locations. To make things more interesting, all the places are extremely difficult to get to. So the parties concerned will be furious when they find out they've been sent on a wild goose chase."

He pointed out the first on the list of hiding places.

Head five miles southeast of Vaumurier, to the hamlet of Gravelle, to the barn on the Dupont farm.

"There is a village called Vaumurier south of Paris, but there is no hamlet called Gravelle or a Dupont farm."

"That's exactly what I wanted," I said. "My plan is for Hans to end up in such disgrace that he's demoted and hopefully sent back to Germany. It will destroy his career."

Claude looked out at the street again, then turned to look at me as I worked.

"And what about you?" he asked. "Are you not putting yourself in extreme danger?"

"Perhaps," I replied. "My plan is to plead ignorance and act outraged as if I had been duped too. I'll shed a lot of tears and look devastated; plead for forgiveness."

"You might get away with that with Hans, but what about the uncle? Are you prepared for that?"

"No," I admitted. "I'll just have to take what comes. Do the best I can."

He sighed and pulled a rucksack off the top of one of the boxes.

"Here," he said, handing me a small vial of white powder. "It's strychnine. Enough to kill him. Just put it in his drink."

CHAPTER 32

I felt as if the strychnine was burning a hole in my pocket as I re-entered the hotel just before six o'clock that evening. The poison would apparently kill someone within fifteen minutes, but it would be a painful death accompanied by seizures. *I can't do it*, I said to myself. *Why not? You killed someone by smashing a bottle over his head.*

Yes, but that was in self-defense.

I went straight to the bar, praying that the General would stick to his regular nightly routine, and asked Sacha for a glass of tonic water.

"Isn't that your friend over there?" he asked as he poured my drink. Emma was seated at one of the tables with a glass of wine and her sketchbook, adding details to her portrait of a young German soldier.

"Umm, yes. But tonight, we don't know each other," I said.

"All right, I'll play along with that. Do I get to know why?" he asked.

"Later," I promised. "If I live to tell the tale."

As if on cue, right on time, the General strutted into the room, heading toward his usual spot at the bar where Sacha would have his glass of whiskey waiting. Just as I had hoped, he glanced over at Emma. A pretty girl sitting all by herself in a bar—how could he resist? I circumvented her table as I headed to the doorway. So entranced was the General that he didn't even notice me.

"Yes, sir, I am an artist," I heard Emma say in her impeccable German. "I specialize in portraits."

"Such beauty, and talent, too!" he gushed.

"Why, thank you, sir." She glanced up at him shyly. "I don't suppose such an important man as yourself would be willing to sit for me? It's just that you have such a commanding presence; such a handsome face. I would love to add your portrait to my portfolio."

Well done, Emma!

"Oh, ho, ho," the General blustered. "Well, if that's what you think, I'd be delighted, my dear! Why don't you accompany me up to my hotel suite? I daresay the lighting would be more suitable…"

I watched from the doorway for a moment to make sure it was all going according to plan. When we had talked about it earlier, Emma had told me she had no compunction about doing the portrait in his room.

"In his *hotel room?*" I had asked. "Are you *crazy?* He'll try to seduce you, you know!"

"I know, but he won't. I have a secret weapon!"

"What secret weapon? Seriously, Emma, you can't be alone with that man. He's dangerous."

"Yes, but I'm smarter. Don't worry, Lulu, I'll keep him out of your way for a few hours, with no harm done."

I had to trust her, so left her to it. With one last glance behind me, I went up to find Hans. Now was the moment.

\\|/

He was sitting at his desk reading when I entered.

"I have some information for you," I said, waving the paper at him with a smile. "I copied it down as fast as I could when no one was watching, so I hope it's legible."

My words sounded so preposterous. *How could he possibly fall for any of this?*

He studied the list and frowned. *Oh, no, he can already see it's a fake.*

"I'm sorry, there's no map to show the hiding places," I said. "They were using a map, but of course, I couldn't take it. Otherwise, they'd have known."

He stood up from his chair, still looking at the sheet of paper. I was just about to start panicking when he spoke. "And these hiding places are currently in operation?"

"I believe so," I said. "It's supposed to be their new escape route to Spain. And those people on the list are the organizers."

Hans looked up from the paper, immersed in his own thoughts. "If I could pull this off..." he said. "If I could shut down an entire escape route on my own...and make dozens of arrests in the process, I think even the Fuhrer himself would be impressed!"

Going to his cabinet, he pulled out a map of France and spread it out over his desk. "I need lists and telephone numbers for all the German administrative offices south of Paris. The French police will have to be involved as well. Get me the numbers for police stations too."

I did as he asked. "Is there anything else I can do to help?"

"No," he said. "Go home. This may take me a couple of hours to arrange..."

I forced myself to kiss him. "Very well. But I'll come back around eight. We could order dinner to be sent up to your room."

By eight o'clock, Hans would have set everything in motion. Then it would just be a question of waiting for the fallout. And for the General to find out what had gone on behind his back. I wondered briefly if I could beg Hans not to tell his uncle that the information had come from me. But Hans would never agree to that, not even to protect me. He would always follow the rules and do what he thought was right. Always.

I rode home, taking pleasure in the still-warm sunshine and the sights and sounds of Paris. For all I knew, this might be my last day of freedom. But at least the Bernhardts were safe, and who knew—if Joséphine stayed out of trouble, perhaps she'd eventually become the concert pianist she was destined to be. And if I'd managed to ruin Hans' career, the world might be a slightly better place.

I took Jacques to the park, then the three of us sat and listened to the BBC news. Hitler had launched a surprise attack on the Soviet Union, we were informed.

"I think he wants to rule the world," said Jacques.

"*What?*" Maman and I spoke at the same time, gaping at him in disbelief. *We must have misheard him,* I thought.

Jacques looked at us in exasperation. "Hitler, of course. Wants to rule the world."

I felt my heart skip a beat, and I quickly wiped a tear from my eyes. *Pull yourself together, Lulu—it doesn't mean anything. He could just be repeating something that he heard earlier.* Glancing over at my mother, I could see that she was just as conflicted as myself. But I had other things to think about—it was time for me to head back to the hotel.

As I approached, I saw that two new swastika flags were hanging from the outside of the building. It was the same all over Paris, not just with flags but also with German signs and posters. You'd hardly think you were in France anymore, surrounded as we were by all the Nazi propaganda.

My hands felt clammy as I looked into the bar area, almost expecting to be arrested and marched out of the hotel in disgrace. It was quiet in there with few customers and, thankfully, no sign of the General. Then I spotted Emma sitting at the bar chatting to Sacha. She looked at me questioningly as I sat next to her.

"So far, so good," I said. "He bought into it, anyway. What happened with the General?"

She smiled. "He's having a little nap right now."

"Nap?" I couldn't help but open my mouth in astonishment. "Oh, good heavens, what did you do?"

"I told him to sit in the armchair, and I refilled his drink for him—with a small additive." She lowered her voice to a whisper. "A sleeping powder!"

"So that was your secret weapon?" I asked.

"Damn right," she said. "It will only last a few hours, but it'll keep him out of your way in the meantime. And look…" She showed me her sketchpad. There he was, true to life, a perfect depiction of the General.

"I could use that for knife-throwing practice!" I said. "Thanks, Emma. I couldn't have done this without you. But now I have to go and see Hans." With a "good luck" from Emma and a wink from Sacha, I left the bar and headed back upstairs.

His face was flushed, the top button of his shirt was undone, and his hair in disarray. I had never seen Hans in such a state before. Even his desk was in a mess, covered as it was by maps and notes.

"Almost done!" he said cheerfully when he saw me. "Louise, I honestly believe I've pulled it off! There are a couple of offices not answering their phones, but most of the men I spoke to were keen to follow my orders. I insisted that the operations should take place under cover of darkness, to add an element of surprise."

Instinctively, I looked toward the window. The sun wouldn't set until close to ten o'clock, which was two hours off.

"I told them to keep me informed throughout," he continued. "I imagine it will all be over by dawn. Then, tomorrow, I'll be able to fill in my uncle. He'll be stunned!"

"He will indeed," I said. "Now, let's order some food to be sent up. You need to eat, and I know you don't want to step away from your telephone."

Half an hour later, we were dining on cold chicken, freshly baked bread, and salad as Hans speculated on the glory that was to be his.

"I could be promoted to the rank of Major. But I might also receive special recognition, like an award or even a medal. And I was thinking when all the arrests have been made, I might insist on the perpetrators being publicly hung. What do you think? Or perhaps just shot. In either case, I would be sure to publicize the event to put a stop to any more of this nonsense."

My appetite gone, I wrapped some bread and chicken in a napkin to take home. "You don't mind, do you?" I asked. "I'll leave you now, as I'm sure you have a lot of thinking to do. But I'll see you tomorrow!"

We said our goodbyes, with Hans, so distracted and preoccupied that he barely kissed me goodnight. I left him to it with a huge sense of relief.

∿

I had no idea what tomorrow would bring, and, tired as I was didn't expect to be able to sleep. But it seemed that no sooner had my head hit the pillow when Maman was shaking me awake.

"Louise, get up!" Her voice was loud, forceful.

Groggily, I half-opened my eyes. "What time is it?"

"It's seven o'clock, but you have to get out of the house. *Now!* He's here for you—the General!"

I leaped out of bed and raced to the window. Two German trucks were parked outside, soldiers waiting with their rifles at the ready. And there was the General, looking angrily up at the house from the street. This was no social call.

"Out the back door! Quick!" shouted Maman as I turned quickly away from the window. She pulled the covers up over my bed. "I'll tell him you didn't come home last night!"

I ran downstairs to the back door, but it was too late. His men were already surrounding the house to prevent my escape.

A heavy pounding on the front door.

"Louise! I know you're in there," bellowed the General. "We need to have a little talk, you and I!"

"It's no use!" I said to Maman. "I have to answer it. Otherwise, he'll break the door down."

Jacques tugged at the sleeve of my nightgown.

"Not now, Jacques," I said. "I'd better open it!"

"No-o-o!" said Jacques. "You can hide! Come with me!"

He pulled me by the hand, and I looked anxiously at Maman.

"Yes! Go! Hide!" she said, and Jacques pulled me into the sitting room. *There's no place to hide in here*, I thought, until the bookshelf that took up almost a whole wall opened up to reveal a hidden room. He pushed me inside, thrusting a flashlight into my hands, then disappeared from view as the wall closed me in.

"Just a moment, just a moment," I heard Maman call. "I'm coming!"

"Ah, my dear Margarite," said the General. "How lovely to see you. Much as I enjoy your company, however, it's your lovely daughter I'm here to see today. We need to have a little *chat!*"

The way he said the word "chat" sent shivers up my spine. I turned on the flashlight and looked down to see Jacques' old teddy bear, Froufrou, on an old baby blanket.

"She's not here, General," said Maman. "In fact, she didn't come home last night, so I don't know where she is."

"Search the house!" the General roared.

I turned off the flashlight as the sound of heavy boots echoed through the house. From the crashes and bangs that could be heard, I guessed they weren't being too careful with the furniture.

"Nothing in here!" said a voice so close the soldier was probably within touching distance.

"Nothing to report, sir!"

Then, silence. I held my breath; heard the creaking of the stairs as someone moved from room to room. *He's doing his own search,* I thought. *Looking for clues.* With a sudden rush of heat to my face, I realized my handbag must be lying around somewhere. Probably right here in the sitting room. Or maybe on the kitchen table. I couldn't remember. If he found it, he'd know Maman was lying. And if that happened, I would give myself up. There was no way I would allow my mother to be punished for *my* foolish decisions.

After what seemed like an eternity, the General spoke.

"When you see your daughter, kindly convey my regards. Let her know that I am anxious to see her regarding a small matter." He clicked his tongue. "Between you and I, it's her *loyalty* that's in question. But thank you for your hospitality, Margarite. And my apologies for any inconvenience!"

A couple of minutes later, Jacques released me from my hiding place.

"They've gone!" he announced.

"You wonderful boy!" I said, hugging him tightly. "You just saved my life!"

But not only had my brother hidden me away in the nick of time, he had also spotted my handbag on the sofa and had hidden it behind the cushion where he sat.

"Good Lord," said Maman. "I never gave that a thought!"

She and I gazed in wonderment at Jacques for so long that he hid his face behind his hands.

"*Stop!*" he said, and we couldn't help but laugh.

CHAPTER 33

Maman was upset when she saw me getting ready to go to the hotel.

"He'll arrest you! We'll never see you again! Come on, Louise, have some sense. You need to leave Paris—we'll come with you if you want!"

"No, Maman, I have to go and face the music. I want to try and talk my way out of it."

"I don't understand," said Maman. "Why are you being so stubborn?"

"Because I want to hold on to my job there. It's just so easy for me to change bits of information here and there when I do the translations—I think I might be saving a lot of lives. And there's so much more potential for the future..." The files in Hans' office labeled "top secret," for example, could be invaluable to the Resistance.

"You realize you're behaving just like Joséphine did, don't you?"

Her comment brought me up short. Joséphine had been fanatical about bringing down the Nazis—and at the time, I'd felt nothing but contempt for her. Now I was behaving the same way.

On my way to the hotel, I decided on a course of action. I would try to avoid the General, go straight to Hans, commiserate with him, claim ignorance, and throw myself on his mercy. Trouble was, Hans wasn't the forgiving type.

I'll just have to rely on my wits. If worst comes to worst, I can make a hasty exit. I also had a little glass vial in my pocket. *And I will use it if I have to.*

At the Lutetia, it appeared to be the start of an ordinary day, business as usual. I was relieved to walk in without being called out by the guard—evidently, there was, as yet, no warrant out for my arrest. I took the stairs rather than the elevator and glanced down the hallway before approaching Hans' office. Not a soul in sight, but then I heard a voice.

I took a few tentative steps down the corridor and soon realized the voice was coming from Hans' office. It was the General. I couldn't make out his words, but then the door flew open. At the same time, the telephone rang.

"Goddamn it!" the General bellowed. "NO! Don't you answer it. Leave it to me! You've done enough damage!"

As I crept closer, the General barked at the person at the other end of the line. "General Hartmann here! Yes. Yes, I know...Well, there isn't much I can do about it now, is there?"

The door was wide open. Standing well out of sight, I peered into the room. As the General stood with the telephone to his ear chastising the caller, Hans stood off to one side with his arms hanging loosely at his side and his head down. He was unshaven and uncombed, wearing the same clothes from the night before. Even from where I stood, I could see the dark circles under his eyes and the despair in his demeanor.

He looked broken; defeated; overwhelmed—with no trace left of the conceited, egotistic, arrogant man he had been. I could almost feel sorry for him.

Isn't this what you wanted?

Yes, but is it his fault he was taught to hate when he was a child? What chance did he have to become a decent human being?

Just as the General hung up the telephone, it rang again. "Goddamn it! Yes, hello, this is General Hartmann! Didn't I just tell you…Oh, sorry, Field Marshall, I didn't realize it was you. Yes. Yes, sir. Of course, sir. Heil Hitler!"

He hung up the telephone and turned on his nephew with a vengeance. I backed out along the hallway to the safety of the stairwell as his words bounced off the walls.

"Do you *understand* what you've done to the family name? You were *duped,* you imbecile! All the time and resources that were wasted last night! A lot of people are angry, my boy, and that includes Field Marshall von Kluge, who wants to see you, by the way…"

Hidden from view, I listened as the General ranted for a good five minutes before leaving the room and heading in the opposite direction, no doubt to his own office. The door to Hans' room closed, and I hesitated. Perhaps foolishly, I hadn't expected such an intense reaction. But now that the General had left, here was my chance to speak to Hans. Deciding to give him a few minutes to recover from his uncle's harsh words, I sat on the stairs for a while, figuring out exactly what I should say and trying to arrange my face into the appropriate expression.

About five minutes must have gone by. I was just about to leave the stairwell when a loud *bang* stopped me dead in my tracks, and I leaned against the door for support.

I knew that sound. A gunshot.

Office doors opened as people came out, looking for the source of the sound. Ingrid, the typist, stood outside Hans' room.

"I think it came from in here," she said.

Then, there was the General, coming up behind her and pushing her aside. He turned the doorknob, pushed the door open wide, and stepped inside.

Ingrid screamed and stepped back.

"He's shot himself!"

It all seemed to be happening in slow motion. I didn't realize that I was almost at Hans' door when the General, ashen-faced, came out of the room and noticed me standing there. With a face twisted in pain, he raised his arm as if to accuse me with a pointing finger. His mouth was open as if he was trying to speak, and his eyes were still locked on my face as he clutched his chest, then fell—first to his knees, then sideways, as his head hit the floor with his eyes still open.

Ingrid screamed again, and there were calls for a doctor. Amidst the chaos, I slipped into Hans' room and quickly averted my eyes. Hans had been sitting at his desk. Most of the back of his head was gone, and there was blood and gore plastered on the wall behind him, even on the ceiling. Fighting the urge to vomit, I looked at his desk for the list I had given him. I didn't think that anyone was likely to investigate the source of the information that ultimately resulted in his suicide, but I didn't want to take any chances leaving behind those notes written in my own hand.

It looked as if he had swept all his maps and papers off to one side of the desk. But there, directly in front of his body, was a folded piece of paper with my name on it. The pen he'd used was lying off to one side, lidless, in a puddle of black ink. With shaking hands, I opened it to see three hastily written lines. My eyes clouded over, making the words illegible, so I held onto it as I found the notes I'd come to find, then left without looking back.

The hallway was still in confusion as I made my way down to the General's office. Scrabbling quickly through the files in his drawers, I pulled out anything that might relate to either my mother or myself. A folder labeled "Informants" seemed like a good bet, as did another entitled "Intelligence," both of which I took to hide away in my own office to read later.

But the letter I'd found on Hans' desk—that I had to read now.

Louise,

I thought you loved me, but you betrayed me. You destroyed me. I fell for your lies.

The shame is unbearable, and I have nothing left to live for.

Uncle knows everything. Don't worry. He will make sure you pay the price.

Shivering in horror, I tore up the letter into dozens of tiny fragments, then did the same with my incriminating notes. *Had he loved me?* I wondered. *Or had he been using me for information?* I would never know the real truth, but somehow, I suspected that the answer to both of those questions was a yes. Yes, he loved me—in his own way, and yes, he used me as a source of information.

From then on, it seemed prudent to behave as if I were numbed by the tragic loss of my beloved Hans and his uncle. I stood sadly next to the General's body as he was pronounced dead and dabbed my eyes with my handkerchief as Hans' body was put on a stretcher and taken to the morgue. When, later that day, the police came to ask questions, I made sure to let them know how upset and shaken I was by the fact that Hans had taken his own life.

"He was such a wonderful man," I sobbed. "I loved him so much. I don't understand why he did this. He had so much to live for! And then, for us to lose his uncle, too, at the same time…it's almost too much to bear!"

Discomfited by my expressions of grief, the police officers were quick to leave with hasty condolences. And that was the last I saw of them.

A week later, however, the Lutetia Counterintelligence branch received a new commanding officer. Newly arrived from Germany, Major Braun glanced tentatively around his new office and looked at me questioningly.

"I hate to ask, but it didn't happen in here, did it? You know, the…"

"Oh, no, sir. This was the General's office. Nobody… umm…died in here."

Hans' office had been cleaned out and left, for the time being, unused. His books and files had been boxed up and placed conveniently in my office in order for me to relocate them as necessary.

The Major spoke hardly a word of French and soon confided in me that he felt homesick. "It's a strange country, France," he said. "And the French people are even stranger. Still, I suppose I'll get used to it eventually. In the meantime, the Fuhrer wants us to take in all the sights of Paris while we're here."

He looked at me beseechingly, and I knew what was coming.

"I don't suppose you'd mind accompanying me, would you, Fraulein Bellingham? With you being able to speak German and French, it would be so helpful." He cleared his throat nervously. "Just as a work colleague, of course! I am a happily married man, as you may know!"

"Please, call me Louise! And, of course, I'd be happy to show you around the city."

"Louise, thank you," said the Major. "It will be nice to rely on someone I can trust!"

EPILOGUE

October 1941

Emma, Jacques, and I are sitting on a bench in the park, watching the children sail their model boats across the lake in the autumn sunshine. Or, rather, Emma and I are.

Jacques informed me this morning that he was too old to be interested in such childish things. He'd much prefer to read his book, he said, and now sits at the end of the bench, avidly devouring the words of Victor Hugo in *Les Misérables*. He's a different person nowadays. Still quiet, often withdrawn, but most definitely maturing. Maman and I have even talked to him on more than one occasion about the day of Papa's death. Conversations that are painful, difficult, and yet long overdue.

"Are we all set for tonight?" I ask Emma in a low voice.

She replies with a quick nod.

Over the past two months, we have set up an escape route from Paris to Spain. Unlike the fake route that resulted in

Hans' shame and ultimate suicide, however, this route is tried and true. So far, with Claude's expertise, we have successfully helped over twenty Jews and three British airmen who were shot down to leave the country. While Emma is responsible for providing the escapees with false papers, my job entails garnering information from counterintelligence, at the same time taking every opportunity I can to undermine and impair their operations with my translations.

To my knowledge, Major Braun has no suspicion of my subterfuge, wanting nothing more than his time in Paris to be over so he can return home to his family. Even so, I'm always on edge, constantly looking over my shoulder, especially fearful of the Gestapo, who are willing to pay hundreds of francs for information about missing Allied airmen or the harboring of Jews.

Maman continues to run her underground newspaper with the help of colleagues at the University. Although she always denies it emphatically, one such colleague has become more than just a friend. He's French, a widower, about the same age as her. He comes over to the house three times a week to tutor Jacques in mathematics and languages and, much to my delight, took Maman out for dinner last night.

The Bernhardts made it safely out of France to England and are currently living at Emma's parents' house in London with a dozen other Jewish refugees.

"My folks are happy to help," said Emma. "They have so much money, they don't know what to do with it. And they like to think they're doing their bit for the war effort!"

Sacha and I spend time together—just as friends—going out for coffee or to the movies. Funny thing, we each know the other is involved in the Resistance but never talk about it. The less you know, the better, as Claude always says. I'm even on speaking terms with Lucie again. She still works in the restaurant and seems happy enough, having found herself another German boyfriend.

The shortages in Paris are getting worse as people slowly starve, while throughout Europe, hundreds of thousands of Jews are being murdered in newly created concentration camps. For us, the situation seems hopeless, but that doesn't mean I'll ever stop trying to bring the Nazis down in my own small way.

As two young German soldiers saunter past our bench, one of them glances in my direction and smiles. How like Hans he looks—tall, blond, blue-eyed, with that inbred arrogance that they all seem to exhibit. Quickly, I look away, ignoring his greeting and sighing with relief once he's walked past.

No new romances for me—my hopes are focused on rekindling an old one. For months now, I've been putting out feelers in all directions to locate Taddy. And just this morning, I received word that a Tadeus Werner has been located in a prison camp near the Spanish border.

And how many Tadeus Werners in the world can there be?

The End

Other books by Valerie Anne Hudson:

Welcome to the Madhouse (Maids of Maddington Series, Book 1)

Love, Lies, and Betrayal (Maids of Maddington Book 2)

A Twist of Fate (Maids of Maddington Book 3)

The Marquis' Daughters: In the Shadow of the Guillotine

Runaway Princess: A Young Adult Historical Romance

Mariposa Mysteries Trilogy

My Friend The Giraffe

Printed in Great Britain
by Amazon

35921951R00143